Californians and Other Cowboys

MARK BISKEBORN

Author:

A Sufi's Ghost

Californians and Other Cowboys

Rivers of Mojave

Sonora Winds

Moroccan Winds

This is a collection of eleven short stories, mostly set in California currently.

In Two Birds of Paradise, we learn that Todd's wife left him after he lost a leg and returned from Iraq. He meets someone at the Los Angeles Hilton who has a lot in common with him. She knows how to ease his worries and make the time fly.

An author of many nonfiction articles published on various blogs or online magazines, Mark Biskeborn has written numerous short stories, and volumes of poetry as well as novels: Rivers of Mojave, Sonora Winds, Moroccan Winds, and A Sufi's Ghost. A new novel is being on the table now. With an MA in Comparative Literature. Mark served two years as an editor, working with various writers and even with Special Forces soldiers who contributed to Intervention Magazine.

Contents

Two Birds of Paradise

"Time we talk," Todd said, before he sat down. They were both staying at the Hilton, corner of First and Main, set along the Los Angeles city streets, lines of concrete and sharp angles. She wore a summer dress with fancy pink lingerie to cover the nakedness hinted at underneath the sheer cotton, especially when she stood against the sunshine. She'd pinned her hair up the afternoon he walked into the Dean Martin Lounge.

"Sit here," she said from the deep cushion chair where she sat most of the day, "next to me." She closed the book she was reading, a finger holding the page, and smiled as he sat dressed in island flower silk shirt and baggy blue jeans.

"You didn't have to get dressed up just for me," he joked.

Her quick smile encouraged him. "I figured you'd be good to talk with."

"Talk?"

"Anything you want, except sports, football in particular," he replied.

"I don't play...football that is." Her eyes flashed.

"You're not the type." He rubbed his hands over his blue jeans.

She eyed him from his shaved head—the weathered look to his face—his athletic build.

"Here by yourself?" he asked.

"Eight months now." She crossed her legs, showing some thigh. "So, now you're what, courting me?"

Her matter of fact talk—he liked the way she said it.

"If you're interested, Lucinda Williams is playing in town this Thursday, down at the Veterans' Hall."

"Love her songs." She wedged the book in next to her hip.

"I like your dress. Style, lady, style."

"For thirty-something? You should see me with a good blond bleaching."

"Woman like you, you can rule this town with a smile and a new dress...no need for bleach."

"Why the shaved head?"

"A habit from the Marines."

"How'd you lose the leg?"

"I went down the wrong road on the wrong day in Kirkuk. What they call 'Improvised Explosive Device.' Damn thing took out part of my intestine and liver and a kidney too. What the hell. Can't live forever. You hang around too long, you end up with

Alzheimer's, like my dad. He gets dressed every day, drives around in his car visiting his lady friends. Then gets lost, can't find his way home, sometimes even has to sleep in his car."

"Where's Kirkuk?"

"You don't watch the news much. Iraq." He rubbed his knee near his prosthetic leg. "What brings you to stay so long here? I talked with you a week ago at the complimentary brunch. You don't remember, do you? I'm Todd. I remember you. Nellie, right?"

"I like it here," she said with a sigh, setting back in her chair. No better reason. What about you? Why're you here so long?"

"It's near the Veterans' Hospital."

"You spend a lot of time there?"

"I stay here now. I like the luxury. Government pays for some of it. I didn't have insurance. Sold my house when my wife moved up to Seattle. Got some equity. I did all right in construction, built rows of houses in the Valley until the Reserves called me back. And back again."

"You joined the Marines. You must have liked it."

"Something like that." Todd let his eyes roam off into space.

"You did the dirty work? Shot people?" She looked him square in the eyes.

"That's a hell of a question." The romance he once sensed in the air crashed down so hard on the tile floor he heard it shatter into pieces.

"You said I could talk about anything except football. Change your mind?"

"Not a subject for light conversation. That's all. Guys come back after a year or more of solid combat, they don't talk about it." Uncomfortable, he teased his black mustache.

"So," she said softly, "you see me, you expect some chit-chat about the weather, maybe the arrangement of those bird-of-paradise flowers over there in the fancy pots?" She nodded toward the big ceramic containers.

"I don't care to talk about it. That's all." He crossed his leg and started shaking his foot back and forth, nerves finding some way out of his system. Memories started seeping in. The ones he tried to push away, better left alone.

"A person who can't talk about something," Nellie pressed him with a cool voice, "it can twist up inside and gnaw away at your heart...pull you into hell."

"Sounds like you speak from experience." His foot still shook, though not as hard and fast as a rattle snake's tail.

"You're still avoiding my question." She brought her left hand up, thumb under her jaw bone, red-hot polish on her long nails, no wedding ring.

"Fine." He stopped touching his mustache and sat up straight. "You want some...some hard core combat stories...a way to pass the time in the afternoon? So I did sign up for the Marine Reserves. I was naïve. You could say, 'well intended.' Once I got over there, it opened my eyes to a whole new world—one where the sewers busted open spewing shit and piss in the streets. The smell...bad enough to close the LA Airport, if it was here. That was the easy part. The dead bodies...dead kids, women...a little girl dressed in a cute summer dress...her legs shredded to the bone; she lay on her back...side of the street dead, blank face looking up into the sky. Cluster bombed. Carnage all over. Artillery always scattered body parts all over the towns we entered. I was a driver...a Humvee...you know? We rolled into Nasiriyrah...turned a corner...right there in the middle of the street an old man's head lying...right there...a head. I swerved but not enough, ran right over it. The sound of it cracking under the tires...that comes back to me sometimes...that sound. The worst, though...when we guarded a road block. Some woman drove up trying to leave the shelled town. We waved her to stop. She freaks out and speeds forward. We had to shoot. Standard rules of engagement...the way we stayed alive. We had to shoot. Afterward, I walked up to the car. The woman was dead. A little girl sittin'up straight in the back seat, in shock...ten, maybe twelve years old. She sits there lookin' at me with big brown eyes. I opened the door and touched her arm to help her out. Top of her head slides off, falls on the ground. I stepped back and put my boot in her brains on the ground and slipped." He fell silent. His eyes, glossy red, returned from some other place and time and looked at Nellie for a moment, and then said, "You asked."

Nellie leaned forward, reached out her hand and glided it over his bare arm and then sat back in her chair. "Not the stories we see on the TV."

"It's like they keep it all hidden. Civilians have no clue about combat. They think it's some kind of job people do...like...like going to the office. The other day I saw in the *New York Times*, they say some six hundred thousand innocent civilians died in Iraq. Think about it."

Nellie sighed. "It's good you can talk. Get it off your chest."

"You're the only one I've told this to." He set his foot flat on the floor and leaned his shoulder into the arm of his chair, closer to her. He pointed to the black and white photo framed in glass hanging on the wall.

"Dean Martin," said Nellie.

"Autographed." He turned his head, looked around. The orange and gold birds-of-paradise opened in full splendor. A silence crept in and floated in the air, mingling with the cigarette smoke drifting in from the terrace through an open glass door at the end of the bar. He cleared his throat. "My dad loved Dean Martin."

"What was he like?"

"Dean Martin?" His lips opened a little.

"No." Nellie chuckled. "Your dad."

"He died years ago, when I was young. He boxed for a year or two while he was still in the Army, Eighty-ninth Division. That's probably why he liked Deano. Dean Martin boxed for a while, you know?"

"Really?" Nellie said.

"Yeah, I heard about it once on the radio. They said Dean Martin's hands were messed up from boxing...arthritis and such."

"And your dad, his hands?"

"Boxing didn't faze him. He was a tough guy, but sensitive inside, you could see it if you looked close. Stoic as an icebox. Never talked about his feelings. World War II combat left a mark on him though."

"How so?"

"You're a curious lady...a great looking lady but curious as a cat."

"Ask questions, you learn things." She smiled. "I purr too."

"I bet you do." He held her gaze for a second. "My dad...carried pieces of shrapnel around in his legs. He'd frozen his feet in Germany. Caught typhoid fever...almost killed him, gave him narcolepsy for the rest of his life. His whole unit was wiped out one afternoon. He barely survived by throwing himself into a cold pond where he could hide."

"He told you his war stories?"

"That's the only one I know. He never talked about it. I asked him about it once. Put him in some god-awful humor. He made one thing clear to me though. No heroes in war. Not so much as a teaspoon of glory. After I came back from Iraq, I understood what he meant. Nobody ever boasts of any mission accomplished. Only the ones never fought in combat turn war into some kind of romance. Fact is, no one ever accomplishes any mission in war. Only a few businessmen win. The rest of us just go home busted up one way or another."

Nellie sighed again and asked, "You think this war will ever end?"

"Eventually...we run out of men or money." Todd shrugged.

"Then what?" she asked.

"I don't know. Probably Iraq will pretty much go back to some Islamic state. That's what it's all about. Church and state are joined at the hip. Islam has its own legal system...government. That's the way they live. Saddam Hussein was some kinda tyrant, but without him, the country is open field for any kind of religious nuts now."

"Funny," she said, "how this got twisted up. Nobody seems to talk about this much."

"That's 'cause it's not so funny," Todd said.

"Well," said Nellie, "you and I, we have plenty of things in common."

"How so?"

"We both like to chat about the essentials."

"I know you were married. What'd your husband do?"

"How'd you know that?"

"Your classy look. Someone's taken good care of you. You're better looking than any woman I've ever talked to. Classy. Elegant figure, beautiful eyes. Hair like silk. What happened?"

"Classic...my ex is loaded, has everything, including a hot little secretary half my age."

"I'll tell you something," Todd said. "You're fun to talk with. Your ex is a sad man. He did a very stupid thing. I've studied the subject. Men are stupid, but I'd say your ex exceeds the average. Damn, you're the finest woman around. What's your ex do?"

"Commercial real estate."

"Here in LA? Maybe I know him."

"New York City."

A lull settled in between the two. Todd glanced around the lounge, at furnishings he'd never been able to afford, expensive-looking pieces.

"You happy here? I mean, living at a hotel?"

"It's a long way from New York. That's all that matters to me now."

He waited before saying, "Are you sad?"

"I have pills."

He nodded. "Back'em up with a cocktail in the evening?"

"Hardly ever in the evening." Nellie pulled herself up in her chair. "Mostly all day long. I mix it up with a little Xanax. Makes me feel like a Buddhist monk, calm. It passes the time."

"I'll get you a drink. What would you like?"

"Vodka, straight up." She smiled and winked. "I've been doing this every day since I arrived."

"Okay, I'll get it for you. I like Jim Beam myself."

"Sit still," she got up and was moving—slim tan legs, nylons with a garter belt. He hadn't seen as much in a long time and then only in magazine photos. Her legs were long and in good shape, her body a golden hourglass. She looked and walked like a dream come from paradise. She returned with drinks in tall glasses, handed him one and settled back into her chair with a coquettish movement that displayed her upper thigh. Now she was looking him over with a naughty smile, and licked her lips after a sip.

"The guys here," Todd said, "either run around for business, or gossip sports...on and on about golf. Or they sit and watch CNN. I get the feeling most of them like G. W. Bush."

"It's just a matter of time with you, right?" She sipped her drink.

"Doctors say six months, a year. What about you? What's your plan? You can't live in a hotel the rest of your life."

"Screwed up my liver. So, they tell me anywhere from six months to 'who knows?' "

"Vodka can do that. You afraid?" He looked her over, admiring.

"Not so much now. The Xanax helps."

"You learn to live with it. Weed is good too...less expensive." He realized how that sounded.

She smiled. "Money helps too. I emptied my ex's account when I left."

"Maintaining that quality of life, huh?" He grinned, finishing his JB. "Only I'm still not used to this; hanging out, not doing much, talking with a gorgeous woman."

"Waiting," Nellie said. "No, me neither."

They sipped their drinks, not a sound coming from anywhere. From the main entrance a beam of light drilled through that somber lounge. She finished her drink.

"You want to get out of here?" he asked.

"What do you mean?" She looked at him with surprise.

"Go somewhere?"

"I suppose we could," she said, nodding her head.

"Or," he said after a moment, "get your pills and move in with me. Room 509. What do you think?"

Nellie smiled. "I've got a suite with a full bar. Living room. Bedroom."

He nodded in a thoughtful way.

"We'll just have to see, won't we?" Nellie took a moment before saying, "Elevators are right there." She pointed with her book. "Let's go up. I'll show you my place."

General Chains

Yellow ribbons were tied around the trees lining Jefferson Street. A banner that said HERO OF BAGHDAD, hung above the entrance of the Washington Plaza Hotel and looked down Eleventh and Michell Streets in Casper, a town named after Lt. Caspar Collins, a U.S. Army officer killed in a battle against the Cheyenne. The town grew up around Fort Casper which served to protect the telegraph lines, pioneers on the Oregon Trial, and the cattlemen who prospered a century ago when the prairies were wide open, once the Lakota and Cheyenne driven out. The banners read across the front of the hotel as a single statement. The day General Chains was expected home after the invasion of Iraq was completed, although the conflict seemed to go on and on. Everyone in town called him General, but officially, he was once a Captain, captain of the high school football team who had worked his way into influential positions of the federal government.

A manager of the hotel and his concierge were the first to notice the colored man who entered the lobby and dropped his backpack on the satin tuck and roll couch in the lounge where it seemed he intended to spend some time. Bold as brass, a tall, athletic colored man dressed in dirty black boots and worn out Army fatigues with a Harley-Davidson embroidery sewn on the back of his black leather jacket.

With the manager standing nearby but not aware that the intruder had entered the lounge near the bar, the young concierge spoke up, raised his voice to tell the man, “You can’t stay here.”

The black man hesitated for a moment, turning his attention to the concierge and said, “Why’s that?”

His calm tone caused the concierge to pause and look over at the manager, who stood in the large entrance hallway nearby, looking out to the parking lot where a Harley-Davidson motorcycle stood at the street curb, its chrome shining in the cold sunny day on the high plains.

The manager looked back into the dark lounge, sizing up the situation. It was hard to tell his age, though he was no longer a young man. Other than his boots, he did seem clean and his backpack new.

"Our hotel lounge," the concierge said, "is not a public place where anyone can camp. It's for our customers. Is there something I can help you with?"

At least he showed his eyes, standing there now sunglasses in hand. Then he said, "I'm waiting on someone, Dick Chains."

"*Dick* is it," the concierge said. "Mr. Chains, he's an acquaintance of yours?"

"We met not too long ago."

"You work for him?"

"You might say."

The manager spoke up, "We're all waiting for Mr. Chains's arrival. Why don't you go out front and watch for him?"

The concierge, whose name was Kal, followed the colored man to the covered entrance area to watch him, backpack hung over his shoulder, walking across the street and down a half block to the Waterhole Saloon. Kal returned to the front desk and said to the manager, "He walked right in here, sat down in the lounge like no body's business."

The manager thumbed through a magazine at the desk.

In town to buy supplies, two ranch workers from the Tall Grass, a range up near Soda Lake, were at a table sipping beer mugs. Wayne and Chuck wore sweat-stained brown hats over their eyes as they sat staring at the blackie at the bar. The bartender speaking to him right there, pouring him a Johnny Walker Red, still chatting as the black man sipped it, nodded, and the bartender poured him another, like they was buddies.

Wayne asked Chuck, "Ever seen a nigger dressed like that with a Harley-Davidson patch on his back?"

With colorful tattoos running up and down both Chuck's arms, he said, "Maybe he belongs to one of them motorcycle gangs."

Once they finished their beers and walked up to the bar, the black man gone now, Wayne asked the bartender, "Who the hell that darkie thought he was drinking in here?"

"You'd think," Chuck said, "he'd go to that bar up near the reservation where the Indians drink their moonshine."

Somehow finding humor in Chuck's remark, the bartender smiling said, "That's Joe Wilson, I'spose he drinks wherever he pleases."

"What the hell?" Wayne said. "He somebody?"

"Joe lives over in Evansville," the bartender explained, "has a house there, went to Iraq in the Marines, now he's back, did four or five tours over there, took a couple a bullets too, got a Purple Heart, maybe some other medal."

"Nobody told me they was smokes livin' around here." Chuck squinted his eyes beneath the low brim. "Least of all any that owns a house and gone to war." Insinuating he held it against the bartender for not spreading the news.

Wayne paused a moment and when the bartender offered no more news, he said, "Chuck's brother fought over there against them rag-heads, only Sam didn't come back like that gangster did."

No more than twenty years old, Chuck nodded his head.

Because Wayne could make no sense of the twisted turn of events, it just boiled his blood. He said to Chuck, "You ever hear of a darkie riding a motorcycle? God-damn, probably a gang member. Jesus Christ." With that, he pulled out his Saint Christopher pendant, which hung on a silver chain around his neck, kissed it, and said, "Man needs protection around this joint."

Joe Wilson walked back up Jefferson Street with a marked limp in his stride, caused by a bullet from an AK-47 or by the Marine surgeon who cut it out. He stared at a large government building against the skyline on B Street, the Dick Chains Federal Building, ugly, but something symbolic about it. Straight ahead up the grade, miles out of town, he saw the familiar sight of the coal fields where his father had worked. In the distance, on the side of the hill, he could make out the main shaft scaffolding and company buildings. It all reminded him of the shaft collapse that caused his father's death just a year before he would have been up for retirement. Two of his father's friends died in that collapse. The union started a law suit against the mining company for breach of safety codes, but the Natrona County judge dismissed the case for insufficient evidence. A sad place, men spent half their lives underneath the ground, buried most of their lives.

With three shots of Johnny Walker warming his belly, Wilson turned back up South Jefferson Street toward the hotel now, looked up at the sign again, HALLALUJAH FOR GENERAL CHAINS, and had to smile, THE HERO OF BAGHDAD, and said to no one in particular, "People believe all sorts'a bull shit."

Moving on up Jefferson Street, Wilson found Washington Park and he could see Highland Cemetery three blocks to the east where his mother and father were laid to rest. When he noticed the bench at the edge of the park, he lost interest in walking over to visit the graves. Close to noon, nobody around, he sat down, pulled a sandwich from his backpack, and ate it. No drummers or band from the Hanover Oil Company to celebrate the home coming, the company mostly shut down now once the wells all pumped dry. The park bench needed painting, the dark green chipping off. Man, but made of oak and comfortable with a little swing in it, back and forth, relaxing. Joe Wilson noticed two young men in a Ford pickup truck driving up slowly, a couple of ranch kids with their cowboy hats.

Wilson wondered how long it'd been since he'd relaxed on a bench in a quiet park—since March 20, 2003, when the invasion began Operation Iraqi Freedom, the Shock and Awe bombings first. In the Fifteenth Marines Expeditionary Unit, attached to Third Commando Brigade, he rode in a closed amphibious personnel carrier across the desert, sitting there like in a tin can in the oven, riding for hours. He stayed there more than two years after President G.W. Bush had declared the end of major combat on May 1, 2003, but that's when things really got busy, urban warfare, civil war, and insurgency. Thinking it'd get easier, he learned it only got uglier and he did more tours of duty.

For days, he rode in the bleaching sun, a road booby trap, what they now call IED, went off, blew away three of his buddies, two of them disappeared in the explosion, only found their helmets and a part of a jaw with a tooth still attached. Despite the setbacks, his unit moved in and took over Port Umm Qasr, moved north, at least fifty oil fields on fire, black clouds of smoke, moved north to more oil fields, got filmed on CNN, moved up Highway 1 through the center of the country to the Rumaila oil fields, then overtook the Iraqi infantry, on to Nasiriyah, got his picture in *USA Today* newspaper, heavy fighting in Najaf and then Kufa, the Iraqi troops defending cities and key bridges along the Euphrates River.

April 2003, Baghdad fell. That's when the shit hit the fan and Wilson took his first bullet, one in the hip, right into the bone, hurting miserably. Gunfights sprung up every day for the extra two years he was commanded to stay on. Later, in a Baghdad neighborhood, he took a bullet in the leg during a street shootout. Before he passed out, he heard the unit surgeon say, "Hang on, man, you're gonna pull through fine, just a flesh wound." Just then another voice said loud to him:

"Hey, I heard you was in Iraq, that right?"

It was one of the ranch kids, talking loud now from the pickup truck pulled up next to the curb. He sat staring at Wilson, who sat on the park bench. Wayne opened the pickup's door, arm hung through the open window, showing how he was so cool. Chuck sat in the driver's seat, fidgeting, tapping his fingers on the wheel. Wilson remembered them from the Waterhole Saloon.

"What'd you do over there in Iraq, latrines?" said the one leaning out the door.

Meaning a black man, what'd a black man do? The kid living in Casper all his life, don't know anything about the world. Wilson was maybe one of the three or four blacks in Casper, a town of fifty thousand whites. The one sitting there squinting at him was a big fella, maybe got his way most of the time or often enough to believe that he could say whatever or use a tone to irritate a person, like he did just now.

"I did what most everyone sent over there did. We did the job," said Wilson.

"Did you cook? Clean things up?"

"What makes you think that?"

"I asked you a question. That's what you did, right? Cooking?" Wayne said.

Wilson paused and decided to stay polite, humor the boy, overlook his ignorance and he'd just go away like a hungry dog looking for a bone to chew. He said, "Marines, combat sergeant, carried an M16 almost always out on patrol, sometimes team leader, sometimes sat turret and manned the forty caliber." Wilson said, "on patrol, we mostly ate MRE's, sometimes back at the camp, we'd do some cooking everyone mostly cooked for himself, sometimes, when we had the time, we'd get together, do a barbeque."

"His brother was an Army Ranger," Wayne said, jabbing one thumb back toward Chuck. "Served in 101 Airborne Division, Screeching Eagles, took over the Talil airfield and got killed in a booby trap—the only way them rag-heads know how to fight. I want to hear what you people did over there while Chuck's brother, Sam, was hit with a booby-trap bomb."

Look at him now, trying to start some kind of fight, not knowing much of anything, shit. Screeching Eagles?

"What? You think I did nothing over there? My fault his brother's gone?"

"I asked what you did."

Wilson thinking, maybe help him out here, inform him, and said, "Karbala. You ever hear of that? It was on CNN a few times."

Eyes half open, the kid stared at him, making a serious look, Wilson thought. Squinty eyed and stupid mean. But you could put one past him.

"What? Some little desert rat town over there, right?"

"Yep, Karbala, Falluja, Kufa, places where it happened. On the push up to Baghdad, ninety-eight Marines killed in one day, mostly the Fedayeen and Iraqi regulars attacked from everywhere, urban warfare in the towns. Over two hundred wounded. Except it wasn't what you say, booby traps, bombs, the Army rode right up to the towns, not knowing where they was going, what was waiting for them. There were men dressed as civilians waving friendly one minute and then shooting the next. What Mr. Chains said about them Iraqis coming out to greet us like we were liberators was all a pile of bull. We were caught in more ambushes than days in a week."

"Jesus Christ, ambushes ain't no way to fight. That's the only way rag-heads would get into it, like a bunch of women. You saying the Army Rangers walked into something like they was dumb?" The ranch worker Wayne said this like it was impossible to believe.

"In places like that it's hard to tell," explained Wilson. "Often enough, they shoulda been doing things different." And thought, why try to explain all this? The cowboy kid giving him another mean beady-eyed look, defending the Army Rangers. He's so proud of the Rangers, why isn't he over there carrying a gun?

"Look," Wilson said in a calm, quiet tone now, "we got over there thinking we'd find WMD's or terrorists, some shit like Bush was claiming, but all we found was a lot of raging Muslims. They'd walk around like regular civilians all the while carrying guns under their clothes watchin for a good time for an ambush." He paused, thought about what the kid said. "There ain't nothin wrong with an ambush if you can pull it off. That's part of war. Only thing, they'd walk around like civilians one minute and then turn into maniacs the next. It wasn't at all what the big men in the federal government said. They lied through their teeth to get us over there. And for what? So they could pay Halliburton to cook our meals, do our laundry? So they could use all those new fangled bombs? They're over there right now pouring tons of cement, building permanent military bases all over Iraq like Bush is gonna be president forever."

A couple more cowboy kids looking like the two in the pickup truck, come walking up now to see what was going on. A few minutes later three more people walked out of the hotel across the street and stood around like they had nothing else to do except listen in on the conversation.

Wilson took all this in, thinking this whole thing through to explain it all from the start, how they pushed north on Highway 1 toward Baghdad, the big bloody battles in all the towns on the way, how some of the Army or Marine units got cut down every time they entered a town. Some of the new recruits, the Army Rangers, no combat experienced, especially not in urban shootouts. The reason why they didn't know shit going into a fight, advancing into hostile neighborhoods, or not knowing what they were doing over there, these guys come looking for some glory, or just a paying job. They got served with street fighters and rocket propelled grenades, no flowers.

If you're gonna get into this, tell the whole story. Wilson was thinking now, how nobody in the towns trusted you. They didn't want to see us, not after all the bombings we done to their towns, killed their husbands, wives, kids with bombs from planes they'd never even seen coming. In day time they'd wave at us, in night time shoot at us. Meanwhile the nation's leaders up in the federal government are telling the rest of the country back home how the

Iraqis'd be cheering us on, throwing flowers at our feet, greeting us as liberators. We went in there believing just that. Most of us went in there thinking we were spreading democracy that is after we learned there never was a trace of WMD's, not single terrorist cell, that is, not until we got there. Then we found out they didn't like us being there and that most of them were dirt poor even though they had all the oil. They were living on camel milk and dates peppered with desert dust because U.S. military services protected the dictators, tyrants, and kings in exchange for good oil prices.

All this went through Wilson's head as he sat there imagining how to put the whole thing together in a few words so that the kids would understand. They'd never been outside Wyoming.

One of them who'd walked up the street must've asked what was going on because Wayne stood up next to the Ford pickup now looking back at Wilson giving his smirk again. The two cowboy kids from down the street stood with their thumbs in their pockets and Wayne with a thumb in his big shiny belt buckle talking. The two from the pickup followed all the others now down the street toward the Waterhole Saloon to get a closer look at the arrival of the important man. Nothing but kids moving from one source of excitement to the next.

Wilson was used to icy piercing looks and looks of hatred or a man staring at him like he was just a spook. He'd long ago learned to ignore it all and go about this business thinking about how it would've driven him out of his wits or put him in more fights than he'd ever seen in Iraq. He sat there waiting a while on the park bench thinking about what he'd say to the man that some of the locals here called General Chains. As a breeze picked up a newspaper that was lying beneath the park bench, it distracted his thoughts and he grabbed the section of the *Casper Star Tribune*, the front page section, yesterday's newspaper. There was a story on the front page:

> Racist flyers decry Mystikal
> By TARA WEISSREICHER
> Star-Tribune staff writer
>
> CASPER -- A white-supremacist organization's most recent circulation of flyers rebukes the rapper Mystikal, who was sentenced last month to a six-year prison term for committing sexual battery on his hairstylist. This is not the first time flyers like these have been distributed. The National Alliance group here is apparently out of Evansville, which is

> right next to Casper.
>
> Mystikal, whose legal name is Michael Tyler, was the featured artist Dec. 6 at Rap Fest at the Casper Events Center.
>
> The flyers were circulated by the local National Alliance, which lists an Evansville post office box as a mailing address and a phone number to Alliance founder William Pierce.
>
> In denouncing Mystikal's appearance here, the National Alliance flyers claim that blacks are committing a majority of the nation's violent crimes and should be chased out of the great state of Wyoming.

Wilson had already received one of the flyers the first day he'd come back to his small house at the far eastern edge of Evansville. He'd heard about creationism, about how God created some men better than others and signaled those differences by the color of their skin. The white supremacists, the National Alliance supported the theory and most of the holy church goers preferred to believe in some version of it, especially out here in the empty plain regions. People filled the emptiness with funny beliefs, their minds like leaves in the wind just reaching for something to hang onto. Wilson was no scientist didn't know beans about Charles Darwin, but he knew a cockamamie story when he heard one and this strange reading of the Bible was one of them.

He moved on to another front page story:

Bill seeks to allow Wyoming hunters to carry automatic weapons
By BEN NARLY, Associated Press Writer Thursday, December 9, 2006
CHEYENNE, Wyo. (AP) -- Wyoming hunters could carry automatic weapons and guns equipped with silencers in the field under proposed legislation that would also allow archery hunters to carry firearms. Sen. Cale Case, R-Lander, is the primary sponsor of the bill. He says he's heard from many archery hunters who want to carry firearms for defense against grizzly bears.

Case's bill, Senate File 79, wouldn't allow anyone to hunt with automatic or silenced weapons. But it would remove the current prohibition against possessing such weapons in the state's game fields and forests.

Wilson chuckled at this new bill. He wished now that the Army would have allowed him to use a silencer on his M16 during the shootouts with Iraqis. He could have concealed his position, avoided getting shot at so much.

It was in a Baghdad neighborhood where Wilson got shot in his left thigh, any higher he'd lost his manhood. As it was, he almost bled to death. He was taken to the Marines dressing station, set up near the Euphrates at a place called "healthy hell" being it was in a fighting area. Wilson remembers holding on to the bedpost, tight, while the surgeon dug the bullet out and he tried not to scream, biting his lip 'til it bled. After, he was sent home back to Evansville at the end of his fourth tour of continuous combat. While processed through Walter Reed Hospital, he saw Vice President Chains, the man the locals here call General Chains, who made a little speech to the wounded and mutilated, saying what they did over there "deserved the unbridled honor of all your follow citizens." Till he came back here to Casper, Sergeant Wilson actually believed he and the other members of the Fifteenth Expeditionary would be recognized as war heroes and maybe find good jobs.

He sat on the park bench waiting and thought more about what he'd say to Vice President Chains if he got the chance to talk with him. He'd ask if he was getting any of that unbridled honor. If

Chains didn't get here pretty soon, Wilson decided, he'd see him another time.

Wilson remembered that while he waited for his medical discharge at Walter Reed, he had plenty of time to kill, he had browsed the Internet and learned a few things about Chains who grew up here in Casper, graduated from Casper High School, became eligible for the Vietnam draft, but got into Yale, dropped out, classified A-1 for military service, arrested in November, 1962, for drunk driving, applied for his first student draft deferment, enrolled in Wyoming University and applied for his second draft deferment, 1964, applied for his third student draft deferment, 1965, got his fourth student draft deferment, graduated from college and got classified again as A-1 for service in Vietnam, by 1966, he married and got her pregnant and got the hardship exception from the draft, in 1968, Chains met Wyoming congressman Steiger and went to Washington where he worked odd jobs for the Republicans, hobnobbed with government officials, got a CEO job with a government contractor called Halliburton and sold equipment to Iran and Iraq, learned the oil business, and moved into the top echelons of federal government. Wilson remembered how the Vice President had shot one of his lawyers while aiming at a quail, and how, if he'd done his military service, he'd have learned to shoot straight.

Wilson now noticed a caravan of black Lincoln Town Cars and Navigators driving up Jefferson Street. Walking back to the hotel, he watched the security agents in the cavalcade. He arrived just in time to move his motorcycle away from the crowd. A solid line of security agents blocked any entrance. "I want to see General Chains," Wilson said to a security agent dressed in a black suit, sunglasses, and a microphone in his ear.

"No one can enter this area," said the refrigerator sized man.

"I know Dick Chains," explained Wilson, "I gotta see him he'll recognize me. We met before."

"The Vice President is in the Jefferson room delivering a speech. Invitation required."

Wilson rode his Harley-Davidson back to his mobile home in Evansville.

The **Iraqi** Woman

Within a few years, when François Lutter would go to confession in his home town, Marseille, a port city in southern France. But for the time being, he would often lie awake at night and imagine how his conversation with a priest would go. Raised a Catholic, he longed to set things right with God. Free him from the heavy burden of the past. Could he plan the visit?

He might tell the priest, “Bless me Father for I have sinned. Haven’t confessed in over thirty years. Since then I’ve fornicated with many women.”

And the priest…the priest…he might say, “Bad women or good?”

He could say, “All good ones, good for me, Father.” He would tell the priest how he had made about eight hundred thousand

Euros in drug trade profits but only maybe a couple hundred thousand Euros in stolen commodities. He would not mention the cash he diverted directly from a couple of cargo trucks in Iraq. All locked up in his deposit boxes at *Banque Nationale de Paris*.

The priest might ask him something about killing. Lutter figured he should say no.

"You never killed anyone," the priest would say, "in all that trafficking?"

Lutter would say, "Yes, but self-defense, not intentional. Now things are different. I retired. I love only one woman, a mysterious woman full of wonder. She makes me want to do good. I'm learning to draw and paint, and garden." He would tell his story, the priest listening from behind the thin curtain in the cathedral's dark confessional booth.

#

Now, in a time before, without a single worry of dying, but with the same caution and zest for pleasures that kept him alive, he observed a woman bathe. From the roof of a cinder block house he rented near the bank of the Tigris River, in Baghdad: he used this spot where he could study the roads, the flow of U.S. Marine convoys. If you were a thief, then your stoop was in the Bab Al Sharji area, a bad part of the city.

She washed at the hand pump that stood in the middle of the courtyard in her small block house. The woman lifted her arms high and pulled down on the long iron pump handle and then scooped water from a large clay basin on the ground. Nearby, corn, carrots, and other vegetables grew in a small garden. Water soaked her long, jet-black hair and ran over her light olive colored skin. He struggled to cleanse herself under her traditional bathing gown, a thin white robe to cover her. It constrained her from pumping the water. She took it off. Nude, her body glistened in the late afternoon under the blazing Babylonian sun. Her young arms were toned and feminine, her breasts large, firm, round with rosy blossoms protruding outward, upward at the tips as if to open and thrive in the hot sun.

When she bathed, he always noticed, sometimes with his binoculars to see closely as she lathered soap over her breasts, under her arms and around her waist, down her buttocks and legs.

Lutter could almost feel her thin waist. He had never seen her husband. He felt sorry for her, for all the women in Iraq. They were all like her, women drying up in the desert heat, waiting for their liberation, freedom, waiting for men who would know how to love them, waiting for a husband to gently caress their skin, massage them, to help them feel deep pleasures. But if the husbands did finally come home…he wondered if her husband existed at all…they smelled of sweat, tobacco, and offered only disdain for their wives' sensuous bodies.

#

Surrounded by a rickety stick fence, a wooden feeding stall made a small corral inside the high courtyard wall, but it was empty and offered no fodder, all dust and sandy soil. So, maybe the man of the house had moved his goats to some other field. Maybe he had a business somewhere in Baghdad and would be coming home soon, maybe with his sons. Maybe there was no husband, no sons. Lutter could only speculate.

The woman looked just old enough to have maybe a young son. Maybe a child stayed in the house. A few chickens roamed the courtyard. Nothing hung on the rusted wire clothesline.

She worked in the garden always alone, especially in late afternoon.

From over seventy-five yards his binoculars allowed him to see her up close. Looking this way now, she stood with her face raised toward the searing sunlight. With his binoculars, his eyes followed the strange lines on her neck running from her ear lobe in spirals down her chest.

Every day in early afternoon she would undress and pump fresh water. That day he waited until she finished and returned into her house before he hurried out his house and down the narrow street. He stood at the tall, thick wooden plank gate to the courtyard garden in front of her house. Through a knot hole he spotted her faint silhouette in the window.

The gate stood ajar by a hair…like some unlocked vault. With a nudge of his finger it swung open wide enough for him to walk through, casual as a man going to pay a visit to a neighbor. Like people do in places such as France.

#

She saw a man with an old military cap on his head, brim bent down to keep off the sun.

Black beard, with the traditional loose fitting white shirt and pants, he looked like just another Sunni in the neighborhood.

She watched him from the darkness inside her house and felt panic and delight at the same time. She tried to form an opinion about him. She had nothing, no weapon, to protect herself.

#

He eyed her there, hiding in her darkness, watching him like a cat in the window without glass, just a square hole in the cinder block wall. He peered into the dark doorway. Closer now saw her dressed in a traditional abaya, a veil that covered her. He never understood this; at best it was good to keep the sun off. Her flowing black hair in the shadows against her black abaya that covered her almost entirely: his eyes strained to find the contours.

He walked up to the door as if visiting a neighbor in Marseille. “May I ask you for a little water? My supplier did not come today,” he said in English.

The woman did not answer him.

He waited a moment.

He stepped back from the doorway like a bee hovering around a garden blossom. He removed his cap and bent down a little to show some form of respect. “François Lutter, pleased to meet you. I live up the road.” He pointed up the embankment toward a haze of heat waves and sandy dust. “I live up there, up the road. I’m your neighbor. Perhaps you and I can know each other?” He waited again, feeling like a fool dressed in the local loose fitting clothes…like pajamas.

“I don’t know you,” she said.

Lutter stood in awe, hat in hand, surveying her raw beauty. She could speak English.

“No, we don’t know each other. My name is François.”

“What difference that make? You come from France? Your accent.”

“From Marseille. I drive truck.” Lutter shrugged. “It pays. It is worth staying in this hell.”

“You should leave,” she said. “You bring trouble. If someone see you, we dead.”

He froze there gazing at her. She came out the doorway at the edge of the light. He felt a shiver when he saw her face and tried to find something to say. He stared at the tattoos on her neck, on her hands, around her eyes.

He became conscious of himself standing in the doorway, silent, gazing into her eyes.

The woman stared back at him in curiosity. Like it was commonplace to see a woman with tattoos down her neck leading to blossoms, a garden. He wondered if he should say something…maybe something like: Those are nice tats. Where did you find such artistry? How to make conversation? The weather? Maybe bring up the price of camels, of dates, or of crude oil? Instead he stood there, silent for a moment.

He couldn't think of any small talk and certain he would never come back to see her again, so he blurted, "How did you get tattooed? Why?"

She smiled; surprised, she moved her head and said, "You are first person to ask ever."

"The Bedouin?" Lutter said. "But you are not Bedouin."

A touch of rage rose in her eyes and voice. She said, “You must go. This is dangerous.”

No fear, only ice cold anger here in the heat of the night.

Someone tried to imprison her behind dark henna designs needled into skin.

“We have met. You introduced yourself,” the woman said, “now leave.”

#

The next day, Lutter went to discuss business. In a more upscale neighborhood, men sat in cafes and discussed everything. Shahbandar was the cathedral of Baghdad cafés. With its vaulted ceilings and brick walls, it was an archeological gem of what some might call a more civilized time in Baghdad, before conversations revolved around the kidnappings that had become epidemic, before the frustrations with electricity that had to improve, before the complaints about the broken gas lines and water pipes.

Antique hookahs were stacked in rows three deep, along with samovars and brass decanters collecting dust. Outside, bookstores lined Mutanabi Street, named for a 10th-century sage, whose phrases the locals often quoted during discussions. Around the corner stood the Qushla—Baghdad's seat of the Ottoman government. As part of the spoils of World War I, it fell when the British and the French drew up maps of the Middle East, defining the borders of countries they invented and when the café was renovated and began attracting the city's men of letters. There was life here, on the walls, centuries of history hung on display.

Unlike most Arab cafés, Shahbandar offered no backgammon tables, cards or dominoes.

In place of time wasting games, men talked—talked a lot—especially around noon, when cigarette butts piled in layers on the floor around the wood framed couches.

Lutter sat with Ali Danif outside on the café terrace in the afternoon shade of date trees where they could talk in private. Lutter asked about the Marines' patrols and their supply convoys. He had been thinking of doing another job. Ali Danif knew where all the opportunities opened; he was connected to the Baghdad network, a loose organization. At one time, they had both worked for a man named Suheil Yassin who knew when the Marines were running currency with their cargo. Nothing like diverting a truck load of freshly minted cash. But those opportunities were extremely rare.

Drive a truck; hook up again with one of his contacts among the Halliburton managers, cut out maybe another truckload of commodities, medical supplies. Just one truckload, he'd be willing to take twenty percent off the top—he wasn't greedy—that was the easiest deal to cut with the managers. He had been studying the roads, he said, when he noticed the strange woman living alone.

"The Bedouin," Ali Danif said. "Everyone calls her that, but she is Iraqi or Saudi. I do not remember the story."

"She lived there hardly a year," explained Ali Danif, "when she went to visit her family in Judaiat al Hamir, her home town on the western boarder. Some roving Bedouins captured the van she rode in. They kept her for months then traded her for some camels and goats…I forget how many."

"That is where she got the tattoos." Lutter said, his thumb circling around the small espresso cup.

"Marked her," Ali Danif said, "with their strange…their own style of obscure Islamic geometric patterns, so that when she die, the spirits see she was God's spirit and not throw her soul out into the desert."

"Better to walk around in this world with tattoos all over you and go to heaven," Lutter said, "rather than have your soul blow in the desert winds."

"No one knows for sure how," said Ali Danif, "but she escaped from that band of

Bedouin and made it back to her house down there near the river."

"Didn't she have a husband living in that house?"

"He almost kill her," Ali Danif said, "left her there and moved into another house here on west side of the city. He left her like some infidel, impure from living with the camel nomads.

No one dare talk to her. Any other husband would have killed her. That is our custom, it is done always here. No one ever talks about the Bedouin to her husband now. He killed a man who asked about her once, shot him in the heart with his pistol."

"So, no one ever talks to her?"

"Francois, you don't know who her husband is. Suheil Yassin -- an important man in the Brotherhood. He owns big construction company. It took a crew a year to build his new house in the Zayouna, high-class neighborhood. Now he lives with three wives, young, one a teenager.

His servant delivers supplies to the Bedouin. She never leaves house. I think he loved her once, otherwise, she would be dead long ago."

"I only caught a glimpse of her at a distance," said Lutter, "but she looks very young, no more than twenty. That house…a prison for her."

"Look at this place…not France." Ali Danif waved his hand. "What choices does she have? She is lucky to be alive."

#

The day had been unusually hot and the winds blew up dust as dark as night. Lutter had tried to work. Ali Danif had told him which roads the next convoy would take, where it would stop, and his contact for the job. But the dust kept everyone off the streets. No one went out, not even the U.S. Marines, bad weather even for civil war, insurgency, and suicide bombings.

He returned home early. He moved his chair and table in front of the window overlooking her house. She never came out, impossible to do anything outside. The dust storm died down only after sunset.

Without a moon, the night fell especially dark. He walked down the narrow road with a package in hand. This time the gate was locked, but he found another door in the courtyard wall.

He pushed it open with a nudge.

The Bedouin gazed up at him. She had been sitting on the porch steps at the back door.

He paused to admire her in silence.

Finally, she said in French, *"La nuit est très sombre ce soir.* You look different."

Befuddled to hear her speak French, he took a minute to say, "New change of clothes."

He wore black slacks and a lime green shirt. The colors hardly showed in the night.

"*Tu parles français.*" He sensed affinity to the mysterious woman now. He rubbed his hand over the black beard he had to wear to look more like a local.

“Yes, I studied in Paris several years ago,” she said in English.

When he stepped closer to the porch, she looked away and into the night sky as if to ponder the heavens, then looked back again.

She said, “This can cause trouble. You should not come here.”

“Why, your husband, he never visits you. He lives in a big house in the Zayouna neighborhood. Why does he not hide you there in the rich part of town?”

She looked away again and said, “They will kill you, they see you here.”

“Your husband’s gangsters? Lock up here. You could live happy somewhere.”

“You should leave,” she repeated.

The dark lines below her cheek bone made geometrical designs behind her ears and ran down her neck beneath her abaya. The indelible lines of henna dye etched into her flesh Tribesmen of Bedouin made concentrated dark dyes from the earth and oils. Its color contrasted against her light olive skin enabling him to see it even in the night.

He bent down to touch her cheek, running his fingers along the lines gently tracing them, following them behind her ear. She raised her eyes into his.

"You are there." He said, "These cannot hold you."

She looked into his eyes as if making some study. "Why?" She said, why come here?"

But she did not move his hand away, leaned her cheek into his caresses.

"I brought you this," said Lutter, handing the small package to her.

She opened it and found a collection of fragrant skin creams, soaps, oil, shampoo, hair and tooth brushes, and ribbons. She lifted a jar of cream and smelled its sweet scent of lavender.

She opened it and rubbed it on her face.

"You must go now," she said still looking into the box of luxuries.

"You are amazing to me. Patient and serene. From last time I came here, I think of you every instant."

"That is why I wear an abaya here, so that men do not think on me."

"I think of how you are. Your skin, your eyes. How beautiful you are."

"You want to lie in bed with me? That it? Now, go."

He sat next to her on the porch steps, put his arms around her waist and drew her body closer to him. He kissed her on the cheek, on the tattoos down her neck.

She moved her head back to open her neck to him. Her lips fell open; she breathed heavy.

"You are so young. You will dry up here and blow away." He kissed her neck, her lips.

#

"Please," she said softly, kissing his lips, forgetting herself, where she was. She felt as if falling, spinning, diving into a dream, floating on a cloud.

#

He ran his fingers through her hair, brushed her long black locks that flowed down her back. He brought his hands around her waist and up, caressing her.

"You must leave. You know they will kill you. You know the customs here. They took me from a car, kept me and traded me for three goats. You must know this. It is normal here.

This is not France. Men kill women here all the time for nothing. I have a radio. I heard the news. Men killed a woman yesterday because she did not wear an abaya. They shot her in the head and then pinned a note on her. It said, 'She was a collaborator against Islam.' "

"Tell me one thing." He spoke softly. "Tell me what you want."

He felt her soft, hot breath on his face when she said, "I do not know."

"Think about it," he said, "think about what you really, really want. I can get you out of here. I have a small plane."

She smiled.

He told her a story he had heard the other day at the Shahbandar café. "A Muslim fanatic shot a man for selling ice. The fanatic explained he shot the man because ice is against Islam…because the Prophet Mohammed never had ice. You see, some things are for religion, other things against it. We spend our lives learning customs and then some priest or imam comes and changes them. It depends on how God feels from one day to next. I tell you something else, if you promise not to be angry to me. Something I could do for the rest of my life, I could look at you, touch you, and love you."

"You are going to leave?"

"When it is time."

"I do not know you. I live alone here for a year."

"You are the most beautiful woman I have ever met. And the strongest. Now you must think about what you want. Then you tell me. I want to go back to France, you with me. I can not live here longer. I want to take care of you."

She rose quickly, carrying the package with her into the house and locked the door.

Lutter returned to his rented house and then went up to the roof where he could survey her courtyard garden. The streets were dark and silent.

The next day, François Lutter slept late and went out at dusk. He drove his old Toyota Camry through the narrow road and parked it down the street from the Bedouin's house. He walked up the street wondering if she had bathed in the lavender perfumed soaps. At his age, he wondered if this young beauty might run off with him. But he let his mind meander through the many paths of his life and onto the risks he took to push open that garden door again. But the temptation, the mystery pulled him there.

He hurried a short way up the street before he noticed two men unloading a box of supplies at the door. He slowed his pace and approached. Old, gray bearded, one of the men wore a shirt stained in a day's sweat. The young man with him completed the delivery. They both stood there, at the side of their small Toyota van, smoking cigarettes. They watched the street from the corners of their eyes, their heads tilted to the ground.

Lutter had not taken more than five steps when the older man spoke to him first in

Arabic, "You don't come closer here." The man took a last draw from his cigarette and flicked the butt toward Lutter.

As old as you are, Lutter thought, *you nurse the warm tobacco in your mouth. The tit of the cigarette reassures you. You need it, nervous about your work...afraid of death.*

Finally, the old man said to him in English, "You made a mistake."

"I do not know your rules," said Lutter.

"Men do not talk with women here. Every man know this. You have not business here."

The old man nodded toward the young man who reached around his back holding something in his belt.

That is all show, Lutter thought. He said to the old man, "I am walking by here, not to this house."

The old man said, "Correct. We break your legs right here. You learn where you cannot walk."

Lutter stepped closer to walk by the old man. Now the old man turned his head to spit and let go a stream that spattered on Lutter's shoe. The sun had set, the street dark, empty.

Lutter was thinking that maybe he worked a job with his man a year ago, driving a truck north to a landing field to move hashish and heroine onto a Cessna Skyhawk. On some other day, he could sit in a café, sip espresso and talk with this man about history, politics. But Lutter saw how the man had thought it would be easy: chase off a Westerner who came sniffing around the woman. He brought a kid around with him to do the lifting, who probably practiced shooting cans off a fence out in the desert with an old Russian military revolver.

Lutter said to the old man, “Do you know who I am?”

“Tell us,” said the man, “so we know who we send to your Christian hell tonight.”

And because he had no choice, Lutter pulled a long assault knife faster than the young man could begin to bleed from a deep stab upward, under his ribcage. Then the old man fell to the ground, throat gashed open as wide as a new mouth without a sound.

Without a blink, not a sound, Lutter dragged the two men into the garden, behind the courtyard wall, beneath the pile of dried wood. Blood oozed into the ground, the garden soil absorbed it.

He knocked.

The Bedouin opened the door and smiled as if waiting for him. She was dressed head to toe in an abaya, ready to leave.

"I am leaving now to take a plane to France…at a landing field in half an hour. Come with me, please." When his eyes met hers, he knew he had yearning and loneliness written all over his face.

She had no luggage, nothing. She followed him to his Toyota.

#

The priest had listened carefully to the story. Finally when Lutter had finished, silence filled the confessional for several minutes. Then the priest said, "You said you love this woman?"

"Yes, father."

"Did you marry her?"

"Yes, father. She is the reason I came to see you today. She is a mystery to me. We live together for many years. We grow old together. To this day I do not understand her. I only know she enchants me, surprises me, makes me want to be a better person. And I try as much as I can."

"Go, my son. Bless you. God has given you a miracle. Go now, forgiven for your trespasses. Blessed are those who love."

Iraqi Deserter

Picture the flat terrain all around except for a low range of hills running north and south, not a quarter mile from the Euphrates River south of Baghdad, near a small town called An Najal. Facing the river, a small ranch stood without any fodder, only spots of dead grass, but mostly prickly bougainvillea and scrub bushes barely surviving in the arid summer. No one worked the ground to keep the irrigation flowing in from the river, a goat ranch without the rancher. A dilapidated stick fence, that once kept the goats in, now outlined an empty range.

Small holes pitted the terrain where mortar shells or rocket propelled grenades had exploded, probably during the invasion: Operation Iraqi Freedom…what they called it. A few dried bones lay around. A hand-pump well stood near a ranch house. Hot breezes scoured the deserted ranch.

Second Lieutenant Wilson surveyed the scene trying to figure out what the hell was going on.

Everybody waited, looking on. Not all in one group, but scattered around. About six men sitting behind the hedge of bougainvillea, impatient shooters who just couldn't stand back at a distance and wait for something to happen. They'd fire at the house whenever the whim came over them or when their commander, Captain Alaa Kata al-Kafage, passed the word they would all fire at once.

Other soldiers sat at a distance on the slope of the low hill, not a hundred yards from the house. They amused themselves, making bets about how someone would shoot the man in the house before he gave himself up.

Less than half the new Iraqi Army Platoon for the An Najal province showed up. Second Lieutenant Kenneth Wilson, US Marines, born in Chicago, often complained about how the new Iraqi recruits would leave their posts.

Newspapers reported how sometimes more than half of a five hundred man battalion would walk off. They would usually come back on the weekly payday to collect their US dollars.

Wilson thanked God he had only a forty-man platoon to command. He had orders to train the Iraqi An Najal Platoon. This morning only nineteen of the forty soldiers showed up for patrol duty. Wilson caught the report about an incident and found the place by lunchtime.

The Iraqis who did come, left their families in An Najal; no woman dared come too far outside protected areas of the town. Soldiers would often take off for a break, alone, sometimes in a small group, two, three, maybe four; they'd walk off, go for lunch to tell their wives what they were doing that day.

No, they hadn't got the man yet. Still inside the small farm house, he hid, not showing his face. But they'd get him. A few more would return to the goat ranch when they heard this news.

Wilson listened and understood most everything they said in Arabic, but couldn't speak it very well. News spread quickly, every little update. They went about their work after nine months of training and after the toughest discipline he could impose on them and still keep them on the job. The training period finished, he passed the command to Captain Alaa Kata al-Kafage. Wilson's commanding officer then assigned him the task to observe their proficiency and effectiveness in situations, combat or otherwise, and write reports on each day's performance.

Wilson shook his head; he'd warned his commander about their training.

Returning from lunch in town the returning soldiers ducked down once they heard the gunfire. They were careful, humping it over the hill toward the ranch, peering to see who reported for duty. The ones coming back after lunch greeted a buddy and ask about Captain al-Kafage. The friend pointed him out. The newcomers made sure the Captain saw them on duty. Not a good day, busy and dangerous, someone was shooting back at them from the house.

The man in the clean uniform, neatly pressed, Captain al-Kafage stood straight and bony, not big but tough like made of goat gristle and hard to kill. His thick black mustache and a long thin nose and large aviator sunglasses mimicked Saddam Hussein's style.

The soldiers would look at al-Kafage, then across the ranch again to the ranch house less than a hundred yards away. Some wood framing, walls mostly brick and cinder blocks supported a roof over a windowless hovel. It set against a low hill where a palm tree stood near the hand-pump well. No tools lay around it to show that someone might live there. The sun bore down on its closed door, chipped and splintered where bullets had driven into or through it.

The man's old car sat abandoned with a flat tire and bullet holes in the windows, off to the left where a small grove of orange trees and palms grew from the underground source by the drying creek bed. Supplies filled the back of the car. The man had bought them in the morning before Captain al-Kafage followed him out to the ranch early in the morning; then he'd called in his new platoon. At least that's the story Wilson heard.

In front of the house, about twenty feet from the door, something lay on the ground. From the slope up the hill, not a hundred yards away, nobody could tell what it was until Wilson pulled out his binoculars. He looked up and said it was a doll made of rags, a stuffed doll with button eyes.

One of the Iraqi soldiers said the woman must have dropped it.

"The woman?" Wilson asked.

"A woman is inside with the man, probably his wife," said al-Kafage, "I don't know for sure who she is. If the man wanted her to stay and get shot that was his decision."

Twenty-nine year old Second Lieutenant Wilson always carried his weapon, an M16.

When Second Lieutenant Wilson finally approached to greet al-Kafage, the Captain didn't shake hands, only nodded and then turned away to say something to his Staff Sergeant Jaafar Mustafa. Wilson stood there not quite sure about how they were handling the situation.

The two men talked, ignoring him. Two of a kind, both cut from the same stringy gristle, looking like father and son. Al-Kafage spoke softly, moving his hands, never smiling, hardly moving his lips. Mustafa stood hip-cocked, posing with his rifle and a sweaty, fatigue hat, nodding up and down listening to Captain al-Kafage, smiling at what he was saying in their private conversation. He laughed out loud while al-Kafage hardly twitched a lip.

Wilson fought the uneasy feeling; a dislike grew in him about how Mustafa stood there with a grin. He'd had to work with too many like him. He tried to remain civil, tried to listen to their muffled Arabic. God, a lot of them worked just like these two.

First Sergeant Hashem perched on a boulder, holding a Colt M16. He owned a café in An Najal, but needed the extra pay from the Army to rebuild his house after it was hit by a stray mortar.

Specialist Mushin hunched on a palm stump smoking a cigarette, aiming the smoke at the front door. Before the invasion, he worked at the local cigarette factory as a packing manager.

Private Madlool squatted and smoked a cigarette next to Specialist Mushin. A truck driver for the cigarette factory, Madlool was one of the biggest Iraqis around, but never offensive toward his fellow Shiites and a chain-smoker.

Hashem was nodding and squinting as if to picture the man inside the house and said, “There was something strange about him. Who has a name like Barham Salih? It’s a Sunni name. Isn’t it?”

“He worked for me in the factory,” Mushin said, looking at al-Karage. “I mistrusted him. Maybe that was part of it -- a name like Barham Salih.”

“Saleh Sarhan,” Captain al-Karage said.

“I hired him,” said Mushin, “had him work two, three months packaging cigarettes…and cleaning machines.”

“His name is Sarhan,” said Captain al-Karage. “There’s no Sunni named Salih. I’ll tell you once and for all this one is a Sunni from Fallujah. He was in the Republican Guard second brigade up north. His name was Sarhan when he killed a U.S. Marine, a Lance Corporal Bryan James, in Qaim while he was fueling his Humvee about three weeks ago and that’s that.”

Captain al-Karage spoke to them as he might address small children. He glared with cold hazel eyes. Probably not the smartest man to make Captain, he led this forty man platoon. And word was out that he’d requested a hundred man company. Ambitious son-of-a-bitch, he never fired a weapon, always stayed back. But they had no reason to doubt him, besides they were all Shiites. Wilson had no say in the matter; he had to follow his orders only to observe.

Wilson kept near Captain al-Karage, the center of decisions. They would discuss the situation and plan what to do. As the American observer after training, Wilson ought to be in on the decision. If someone arrested Saleh Sarhan or Barham Salih or whatever his name was, then he should at least observe the procedures.

"Wait for Salih to give up then arrest him," said Wilson.

"If he isn't dead already. Specialist Mushin."

Wilson stepped toward the former packing manager, who glanced back at him but then stared over the range, not listening.

"What if he's already dead?" said Wilson, "This man you call Saleh Sarhan or Barham Salih or whatever."

Specialist Mushin, standing heavier and taller and at least fifteen years older than Wilson, said in his rough English, "Why don't you go down there and ask him?"

"That's just it," Second Lieutenant Wilson said, "if he's already dead, we'd be standing out here for a while, right? And all this for nothing."

Staff Sergeant Mustafa adjusted his fatigue hat, something he did often, grabbing the baseball-cap type brim, tugging on it between his index finger and thumb and pulling it low over his eyes. Then he shifted from his cocked hip to the other. "This American here, he got better things to do," Mustafa said in his English and laughed, "…busy American."

"No," said Wilson. "It's this Sarhan. Is he dead or alive? If he's alive, maybe he wants to give himself up. He's outnumbered, no way out for him. He's had plenty of time to think about it. What if—" None of them listened to him, least of all Mustafa.

Captain al-Kafage and First Sergeant Hashem ambled down the slope to the grove of palm and orange trees offering shade. Early afternoon then, hot, the air settled.

Wilson wondered if he should follow the two men. He heard a couple of other men talking; he could only make out part of what they were saying, something about a dangerous mission, a day when they fought bravely against the heavily armed Sunni deserter.

Down on the grazing range, dusty and sparsely covered with weeds, thistles and prickly brush, the sun showed its clear light down to the wooden door of the little ranch house where a shadow was growing out from the house and the small hill behind it.

Someone on the slope behind Wilson must have seen the door open. Someone shouted and Wilson and everybody on the slope looked down. The woman had already reached the corner of the house. She stepped out of the house, toting a ceramic pot toward the old hand pump. Like nobody's busy, she walked right out there, beyond the shadow of the house toward the pump.

Nobody took a shot at her; pointing a gun at a house and aiming at a woman were two different things. No one knew who she was. They weren't after her. None of them knew what to make of her.

She knelt down, put the pot under the pump and worked the handle, out in the open. Then at a casual pace she carried the pot full of water back to the house; covered head to toe in a black *abaya.* They could see only parts of her face, the slats cut open for her eyes.

Did the man send her out? Wilson thought. In any case, he was alive, wanted to stay that way. *She had a lot of nerve...going about her chores like nothing.*

Maybe she should just go about her day…screw the platoon and all their guns pointed at her; she did what she considered her duty like the rest of them. But she didn't count much, not here; the man could lose the woman and get another one. Maybe he already had another one, maybe two more.

Captain al-Kafage didn't look at Sergeant Mustafa; his head moved along the same path where the woman now pranced back to the house, but he must have known Mustafa was right there next to him, holding up his rifle.

"She's walking like she wants to tell us something. She don't give a damn about you and your rifle," said Captain al-Kafage.

Mustafa pressed the butt of his rifle against his shoulder, pulled the sights on her. "Shoot her?" he said, as if hoping the answer was yes.

"Just give her something to jump and dance about," said al-Kafrage.

Wilson yearned to walk over to them, take charge. But his orders were to observe, report back on their performance.

Mustafa fired. Dust kicked behind the woman. She never looked up the slope. He fired again and again. He put a couple right behind her feet. His last bullet plunked into the wood door just as she opened it. That was when she pulled the door open and turned, looked up the slope as if to defy him.

Specialist Mushin laughed and said, "She mocks you."

"I wasn't aiming to shoot her," shouted Mustafa back at Mushin. "If I wanted to hit her, she'd be on the ground now," Mustafa shouted.

During all this shooting, Wilson sprinted over to the grove. He approached Captain al-Kafage and asked, "Are you sure who the man is?"

"I explained it to you," said al-Kafage, "he killed an American soldier, Brian James. Sarhan came out of a store, stole a crate of oranges from a truck parked outside. The American saw him. So, he shot the American, afraid he'd report his theft. He had a Kalashnikov, probably used it when he was in the Republican Guard, and he drove away in his car, the one parked over there, next the house. That woman rode with him."

"You say this all happened when?" said Wilson, holding al-Kafage in the eyes.

"A few months ago, he was a private in our company in An Najal too, but deserted."

"But you never talked to this man?" Wilson asked, looking him in the eye.

Captain al-Kafage eyed the house and when Wilson posed his question, he turned and stared at Wilson. That's all he did—just looked at Wilson deadpan.

“We have to be sure about this,” said Wilson. “We can’t just shoot at a man.”

Staff Sergeant Mustafa and Captain al-Kafage turned to him. “We?” Mustafa smirked. “When we need your help, we’ll ask.”

Wilson just nodded his head, not saying a word, and not liking this observation job one bit. In fact, he didn’t like giving training. He hadn’t signed up for this shit…tried to do his job right.

For a second his mind wondered off…a while ago, he went out on many missions just before the full invasion of Iraq. By the age of twenty-three, he went out in a team of ten to twelve men doing reconnaissance and special strikes on strategic targets throughout Iraq.

A Recon Marine, he’d learned the arts of stealth, cunning, and quick kill. One of the first to enter a series of towns up the Euphrates, his team identified areas of resistance and called in aerial strikes. His team charted the path for the invasion. At first so proud to serve his country, he now saw the politics behind it all. He and his buddies weren’t much more than security guards for the black oil pits. Working now as a trainer, at first, was his idea of taking it easy for a while, but it turned out a source of nerve slicing frustration.

Wilson hurried across the range and paused on the palm tree stump where a late sun ray shone on him. He wanted to set this situation right. Normally, he collaborated with a couple of his colleagues from his team whenever he patrolled with this platoon. But today just too much fighting erupted, the Marines were stretched thin, especially since the Iraqi soldiers kept their own willy-nilly schedules. Then the civil war broke out.

Wilson instinctively humped it back over to the grove and heard First Sergeant Hashem saying, "The shadows are getting long. What do we do when it gets dark?"

Staff Sergeant Mustafa called out to the other men sitting around the brush, "Spread out around the house, make a tight perimeter. The man comes out, take him down."

For a while none of the others moved; nobody wanted to take a bullet.

#

"Where is he going?" asked Mushin.

Everyone stopped doing whatever kept them busy.

"Hey Wilson!" Mustafa shouted. "Where are you going?"

Wilson had already entered the range along the stick fence. He just kept marching straight toward the house.

"Wilson!" Mustafa shouted.

Raising a hand to silence Mustafa, Captain al-Kafage gawked at Wilson. He shook his head and took off his sunglasses now that the shadows covered over him, pulled a cigarette from his shirt pocket and motioned for Mushin to light it for him.

"Look at that," said Mushin, with a tone of surprise.

"He is not as smart as he looks, US Marine and all," Mustafa said and jolted when al-Kafage touched his arm and said, "Come with me and bring your rifle. They hustled from the grove and out to the grazing range and sat down on a small pile of rocks not forty yards from the house.

#

With his M16 pointed down, Wilson approached the front of the house. He paused a moment and studied the rag doll on the ground. It had a strange expression on its face, mouth sewn in by thick red thread, twisted by the way it sprawled out on the sand, its legs stretched out over a patch of weeds. Its button eyes seemed to stare up at him in disappointment.

He hoofed it right up to the front door; his eyes fixed on the metal latch, searching to see if it opened just wide enough for a gun barrel to point out. He worried that the man might be aiming at him, waiting for him to come closer.

Now he saw all the bullets lodged in the thick wooden door, pieces broken off in chips, fifty or sixty bullets stuck in that door, the tail end of them showing out of the rough surface like lead nails hammered in. Some holes showed clear through the wood where some of the bullets passed through.

Figuring out what exactly to do, he considered the door…completely closed. He moved in close and did what seemed normal. He knocked just like one rancher going to visit to another, just like back home, Colorado. Then Wilson thought for a second, he'd moved from Chicago, got a tiny ranch in Colorado; God how he wanted to be there right now.

The door opened and a thin man with a thick black mustache filled the open frame, standing there dressed in a dirty, sweat soaked white shirt and baggy dark pants, holding a U.S. issued M16 at his waist, pointed and cocked.

They stood sizing each other up, Wilson close enough to block any clear shot from the men behind him.

"If you raise that," the man said in slow Arabic, nodding toward Wilson's gun, "I can kill you first."

With his free hand, Wilson motioned with his thumb over his shoulder and spoke in his rough Arabic, "Man there says you killed an American a while back at a gas station where you stole a crate of oranges."

"Man's name?"

"Alaa Kata al-Kafage: A Captain in the new Iraqi Army. Says you're a Sunni, served in the Republican Guard and then in the Iraqi Army and that you deserted."

"I don't know the man. He says a lot of things, too many things. Never heard of him."

"He says your name is Saleh Sarhan."

"My name is Barham Salih. The cigarette factory in An Najal employed me before it closed down. Then I served a year in the Iraqi Army and got a discharge."

"Do you have papers to prove your name? Prove your discharge?"

"In my car." He nodded toward his car.

"If I bring Alaa al-Kafage to your door, can you talk with him? Show him that you are not Saleh Sarhan, that you served your year?"

"Those men behind you, they are all Shiites here around An Najal. They've been shooting at me all morning. Just look at this door…full of bullets, some went through the cracks. Shiites," he spit on the ground between them.

"Why did you run from them this morning?"

"They came running, shooting at me. No questions…just holes in my car. What would you do?" He lowered his gun from his waist, pointed down at the ground now, his panic tired brown eyes staring into Wilson's.

"All right," said Wilson, "where in the car?"

"Glove box."

"Okay, I will show them to Captain al-Kafage." Wilson nodded. "Keep your gun down. I'll straighten this out in a minute." He took several steps backward, his eyes holding on to Barham

Salih's. After ten steps backward, Wilson turned, walked toward the car, and looked along the range fence where he found al-Kafage and Mustafa sitting, waiting. As soon as he was out of the line of fire, Mustafa raised his rifle and took a shot carefully.

Wilson looked back at Barham Salih who spun around at the force of a bullet and fell into the house.

Wilson shouted to Barham Salih in Arabic with his American accent, "They weren't supposed to do that."

Laying belly flat on the floor, Salih carefully set his sights on Mustafa and put a bullet through his head.

"Don't! Don't shoot!" Wilson shouted but then saw Mustafa roll over flat on the ground. Then he pulled up his M16, aimed and fired a sure one at Salih whose head fell face down, flat on the floor where he lay in the door way.

Everyone ran to the house, passing by Mustafa who lay dead, to have a look at the Sunni corpse. The soldiers entered the house where they found the woman flat on her back, dead, a rifle shoot in the neck. Under her robe, they discovered that she would have had a child in two, maybe three months.

From the car, Wilson watched as the soldiers made way for al-Kafage the last one to enter the house; he looked down at the Sunni.

A couple yards from the front door, Wilson squinted at al-Kafage, saying, "So, he's not the man. He's not a deserter either." He held up Salih's discharge papers.

"He was a Sunni though," said Mushin, "you ask me, that's reason enough."

"Wilson," said al-Kafage slowly in Arabic so he would understand, "you killed the wrong man, but he did kill one of my men."

Wilson stared at al-Kafage for a moment, not sure what to do or say about this, restraining an overwhelming urge to bust him upside the head.

Then Captain al-Kafage said in English, "But it's like you Americans say, this democracy…a messy business. Rumfeld…your boss in White House…I heard him say on SeeNN."

The Rancheros

Marta drove in her beat-up Toyota Corolla to the King Ranch, one of the largest, most famous in South Texas. Once off the county road, the ride on the gravel driveway stretched out more than five miles across flat grassland browned by the summer. Open fields spread out under an uncompromising sun for as far as the eye could see. Endless low hills rolled little higher than coastal gulf waves. Drying blades of grass glistened like water. For a moment, her head reeled with a touch of dizziness like seasickness, as she drove.

She had learned that Mrs. Bein needed a new maid when her previous one, Ofilia, quit because her husband's job moved to Phoenix. When Mrs. Bein put word out in the Kingsville beauty salon, Haute Coiffure, that the position was open, as Ofilia's friend, she was the first and only to apply.

She had left the Nuevo León district of Mexico together with Ofilia when they first came to the Corpus Christi area about three years ago. They had come to Texas as brides to American citizens who found them through a matrimonial Web site, Sweethearts dot com. Her husband, Mr. Raserei, worked as a warehouse receiver until his death only thirty-two months after their marriage. The word at the salon buzzed among the local ladies that Marta's husband may not have died accidentally. She needed a new job, preferably outside town, ideally outside the county.

Marta had mixed feelings about working for a woman named Mrs. Bein, wife of Mr. Bein one of the owners of the eighty thousand square acre cattle ranch that sprawled over four counties just south of Corpus Christi. It surprised her that the woman didn't fit the image of a Mrs. Bein, and that she was standing out on the front porch.

The slender, long-legged brunette in a shear, tight fitting two piece yellow work-out suit, large Gucci sunglasses and with a broad smile asked, "Martha, as in the Saint Martha, the saint of housewives?"

"No, Marta, da Spanish pronunciation." She replied and then asked, "You out here all alone today?"

"That's why you're here. I need help with the house," said Mrs. Bein, her brunette hair curling over her shoulders. "Come in, please," she said, guiding Marta through the hacienda filled with colorful ceramic floors, vaulted timber ceilings, bronze statuettes of cowboys and Indians on horseback, and paintings of Texas plains. They moved on to the swimming pool, where they sat on cushioned patio chairs in a garden of cacti, lavender, sage and other desert plants. Bougainvillea vines grew wild and wrapped around the cyclone fences that protected the gardens from coyotes and other predators.

A large bottle of Coca-Cola, empty drinking glasses, cigarettes, and an ornate silver lighter lay on the oak table. Mrs. Bein lit a long European Silvest Sylvia brand cigarette and held out the pack.

"For my resume I brought dis profile, Mrs. Bein." Leaning forward, Marta placed her bio sheet on the table.

Mrs. Bein read, "'Romance and love—a click away.' Where did you get this?"

"No resume. Is my profile from a Web site where I looked for marriage, Sweethearts dot com, where my husband found me. Is for you to see my information, all da same except my age, now thirty-two."

Mrs. Bein looked no more than twenty-five maybe less, though she was probably a little older, her expensive beauty creams and pampered life keeping her young. She reminded Marta of a fashion model whose name she could never remember, da one always on the cover of *Cosmopolitan* magazine, who married dat actor, Gear or Grere or someding.

"Your English is good, no smoking, no drinking, no children. You didn't have children with your husband?"

"No," she said, offering no explanation, but adding, "I drink a little now with friends."

"But you're not married now?"

"No, he came to Monterrey, Mexico…visit me where I lived. Sweetheats dot com makes the parties when the men come. I dressed nice to meet him."

"He must've liked you," said the brunette. "Marta, how would you like to work here?"

"Si, si, is a beautiful hacienda, big ranch. Mr. Bein is important man."

Mrs. Bein looked back at the bio. "You're religious, hardworking, honest, and church going. Looking for a man, well established, gentle, and loving. Was that your husband?"

"Si," she said, "a good man, except when he drank den he acted mean. I had to stay away because only a few beers made him want to hit me and he was strong too and beat me sometimes. For a man his age he swung a hard fist. He was sixty-four but tough."

"Is that why you divorced?"

"*Aye, caramba*, divorce, I would not do dat, a sin. I am Catholic." She made the sign of the cross over her breasts and kissed her fingers. "No, he died."

"So, tell me, how did he die?" the brunette asked, elbows on the table, and leaned toward Marta. "Ofilia said something about that, I don't remember exactly."

"An accident. They found him beneath a pile of inventory. Boxes of building supplies fell off his...*carretilla elevadora*...uh...his fork...lift." Marta bumped the ashtray on the table as she raised her hand to brush back her long, black hair.

"Was it an accident?" asked Mrs. Bein, her eyes focused on Marta's.

"Yes. He was working alone in a large warehouse," she said.

"The police talk to you, ask you questions?"

"Yes, dey say…an accident."

"Didn't they ask you questions, I mean suspect you of something?"

Marta sized up the other woman. The notion crossed her mind that the brunette might read psychic energy like the old ladies in the Nuevo León countryside. More likely Ofilia talked too much.

"The police met with some of my friends from Mexico…questions as maybe dey do something."

"Were they dealing drugs?"

"My husband was too old for drugs." Marta waved her cigarette to dismiss the idea.

"So, there was no reason for anyone to kill him…an accident," said the brunette holding Marta in the eyes and with a smirk on her lips.

"Yes, an accident," said Marta, "but my sister-in-law, she told insurance company dat I had my Mexican friends kill him. He drank one day and pushed me hard to ground. I no walk for two day." Marta put her hand on her hip and straightened out the bright green summer dress over her long, tan legs.

"Your friends, the ones from Mexico, did you tell them about that?"

"In Kingsville everyone know, and my husband's sister talks a lot at beauty salon, Haute Coiffure." Marta smashed her finished cigarette into the crystal, star-shaped ashtray.

"Well, then, maybe they did do it." Mrs. Bein said this like she wished it so.

"I not know," said Marta slipping another cigarette from Mrs. Bein's pack, sitting back in her chair, focused on the swimming pool glittering in the sunlight. She lit it, blew smoke into the sky. Three men at the far end of the backyard cutting brush and building a shed near the fence caught her attention. "In Corpus Christi, I work for Mrs. Connelly, in her cleaning service. I cleaned businesses, beauty salon, motel sometime. I cook too, Mexican and Italian and some French plates. I keep your house clean and take care of your dirty laundry."

"Why don't you work for Mrs. Connelly any more?"

“Call her,” said Marta, “she tell you I work hard, reliable.”

“What happened? If she liked your work, why change?”

“After my husband died, everyone in beauty salon talk about me. It bother Mrs. Connelly for her business. Maybe you hear stories too, no?”

“You were married almost three years. So you have legal residency, right?”

Marta nodded, drew on her second Silvest Sylvia, and wondered why all the questions, worrying a little now about getting the job.

“It’s a full-time job, you know?”

“Yes, *una casa hermosa*… a beautiful home.”

“When you fill out the forms, put down that you work for Mr. Bein, King Ranch, and I’ll make sure you clear five hundred per week.”

“Very good of you… good money. I work for Mr. Bein?”

“Did Olifia tell you anything about him?”

“She only say that he is away working most days,” said Marta.

"Olifia was a perfect ten, just the way Jorg likes them, slim, young. You know how to ride a horse?"

"Yes, we had a horse in Nuevo León a long time ago. I love to ride but have not in years. Who is Jorg?"

"Mr. Bein. I never ride. He thinks it's because I don't know how, but that's only what he thinks."

Marta looked back now at the three men cutting the brush.

"Don't worry about them. I keep them under control. They look down at the ground when they're around me and don't talk unless I ask them to. When I dance and do my workouts here on the patio, I let them watch sometimes, but they stay outside the fence. Every morning I put on rap or hip-hop, and jazzercise to the music. I know they like to watch me bending. Men are all the same. When I bounce around and stretch to Pup Daddy and Dudley Doggy they stand at the fence pretending to work. They all like to look at the same things, so, I give them a little eye candy in the mornings. Maybe each one sees differently though. They make me laugh. Men, always watching—they work mainly out on the ranges and leave at five every day. When Jorg comes to the patio, he likes to walk around nude. I don't know why, maybe a cowboy rancher thing. I hope it doesn't offend you. Did Ofilia talk to you about me? If so, what'd she say?"

"She said it was great to work here. She said she was sorry her husband…job made them move on to Phoenix."

"I bet that's not all she told you."

"Yeah, she say something like you dance."

"A stripper. I started out at the Body Shop in Seattle when I was barely seventeen, then Hollywood, then in Houston for a year. I moved up the food chain fast, dancing in the high-end joints. Leggy Ladies in Hollywood and the Rancheros in Houston, and I was the top in sales and tips. I brought in the high rollers, sometimes doing over a thousand in tips a night in lap dances and VIP rooms. Jorg would come in with his two brothers, all stiff in their suits and ties, trying hard not to look too interested, a lot of his politician friends—congressmen, senators, governors, all of them republicans around here, and other buddies in business. He and his brothers own this ranch too. The first time he slipped a hundred dollar bill into my panties, I gave him a dirty little voodoo dance, made his woody stand up straight. I told him, 'You must be a rancher, bull horn like that you'd have to take care where you walk not to poke someone.'

He laughed loud when I said that. He kept coming back, two, three times a week for a month, and always asking me out on a date. Finally, I let him take me out. Then I was Mrs. Bein."

Marta listened, occasionally nodding her head, still on her second Silvest Sylvia.

Sitting back relaxed, the brunette kept telling her story. "I was twenty-three and he was fifty-five and handsome, and drove a convertible Mercedes SL500. His first wife died only a few weeks before he met me."

Silence filled the air for a moment and then the brunette said, "Oh, also, Jorg will want you to serve drinks when he has his friends over. They sit for hours and talk on and on about business and politics. Jorg's second cousin is a lobbyist. She has the Armstrong Ranch just south of here. She brings home over a million a year, never went a day to college. All she does is influence elected officials in their decisions, things like government contracts, businesses who supply the military. When I was dancing I know I was influencing men too, but I didn't have a big ranch to invite them over, take them out quail hunting, but I could do that kind'a work too. I went two years to a college…junior college…got an Associate

Arts Degree in anthropology. Then my dad died in that war, Desert Storm, and I got derailed."

During moments when the brunette paused, Marta would nod her head or say, "uh-huh," to show that she was paying attention.

"When you serve the drinks, he'll want you to dress nice. He likes short skirts with nice pantyhose or stockings. You know what I mean?" She didn't stop for Marta's answer. "They come here, him and his cronies, and I help entertain. All I have to do is smile…talk some about the ranch, weather, and such. You watch them closely. They look at each other trying to remember if they maybe saw me working in the strip joints in Houston." The brunette paused to pour a glass of Coke.

"I buy nice skirt?" Marta asked.

"We'll go to the mall, shopping. I'll buy you some nice things, the sort of thing he'll want you to wear. I told you how his first wife died?"

"I heard about it at da salon in town."

"She fell off a horse, broke her neck, out there riding all alone. The ranch workers found her. That was almost a year before I moved in. Before the accident there was some tension in their marriage. He confided that much to me."

The brunette didn't offer details but said, "What color you like to wear? Black or dark shades are good for his cocktail parties. You have large breasts…and leggy with a tight butt. Size 10, right? I know where we can find fun things for you to wear. You'll love it."

"Good of you, Mrs. Bein."

"Whenever we're around other people I want you to call me Mrs. Bein, but when we're alone, you call me Kate like my friends. You and I can have fun together."

#

The next day, the brunette drove Marta up Interstate 37 to the River Center Mall in San Antonio. On the bank of the San Antonio River the shopping center offered everything imaginable, including the big IMAX Cinema. Her new boss took her to the expensive stores, bought her short skirts and spent a lot of money at Victoria's Secret on fine lingerie, more short skirts and dark shear blouses. She took her to the finest beauty salon where they both enjoyed facials, pedicures, manicures, and massages.

Back at the ranch, dressed in her sexy clothes, Marta vacuumed the floor, feeling a little like she worked in a strip joint.

That evening they sat together out on the patio, Marta mixing up margaritas when Mr. Bein didn't come home. They had drinks and tasted caviar and lobster tequitas. It was nice to be friends with a woman who lived in luxury, but Marta waited, expecting the beautiful brunette had something special to talk about.

As the weeks went on, Marta grooved into a comfortable routine at her new job. She cooked, using all the best ingredients for the finest Mexican dishes. Sometimes she made delicious Italian plates, fresh gnocchi that she'd knead from potatoes, cream, and flour.

She ate often with Kate because Mr. Bein seldom came home and when he did, he'd stay only to sleep in the afternoon while floating in the pool on a bright yellow inflated mattress. He'd swim naked just as her boss warned, and he'd often stare at Marta with a big grin while she dusted the statuettes, tables, and shelves.

The setting reminded her of her home in the Nuevo León countryside where the ranches spread out for miles and wealthy, aristocratic men, owned all the land, and invited the elected officials for dinners and banquets. Near Monterrey City, she once saw Presitente Vincente Fox drive by in a cavalcade of black Lincoln Town Cars, paying a visit to Senior Diaz, one of the wealthiest landowners in Mexico and former president who now did consulting work for Ford, Toyota, and Coca-Cola.

After dinners and over cognac, the brunette would tell her about how boring life was out on the big ranch.

"I'm a trophy wife. My job is to entertain during cocktail parties and promote Mr. Bein's business. What can I do? He doesn't allow me to see my old friends."

"Let's go shopping every day, if you like," said Marta, thinking that by old friends Kate meant her *amigas* in the strip joints. She sat next to her new friend on a couch on the terrace.

"That gets old."

"Let's watch TV."

"That's not a life."

"Your husband comes home often enough. You go out and have fun with him," she said, looking for *una solución*. She moved closer to Kate and slid her arm around the woman's shoulders to console her.

Kate leaned close to Marta, rubbing her cheek on her neck.

"He has a girlfriend...several girlfriends," whispered Kate. "I was hoping he'd take some interest in you. Maybe he'd be home more often. Men always dream of having two women."

"At his age?" she said, trying to console Kate, ignoring the suggestion about her being one of Mr. Bein's women.

"He's out with his friends all the time in Houston. He has a condo and doesn't like me to go there. It's his bachelor pad where he brings his girlfriends. I know it. He leaves all sorts of signs there, panties lying on the bed, a bra on the couch. He does it on purpose so I don't go there."

"It's a problem with powerful men. They have too many choices. They forget to love." Marta crossed her legs and shook her foot in a nervous to and fro.

"Yeah, like your husband. You said he wasn't wealthy. Men get bored with their wives and like to look around. Then the wife turns up dead, falls off a horse, breaks her neck." Kate turned to Marta.

They embraced each other and then Kate kissed her on the cheek first. Then they kissed softly on the mouth. Marta's heart beat fast and dizziness spun her head a little as Kate kissed her now down her neck. Marta moved her arms away from Kate and pushed back her silky black hair, warmth filling her neck and face.

"That is why you don't ride the horses," she said, sitting up straight.

"It's so nice to have you here with me," whispered Kate.

"I love spending time with you too," she replied, reaching for one of Kate's European cigarettes on the coffee table.

Kate stood and poured a little brandy in two glasses. Then, she handed Marta one of the glasses saying, "I don't want to finish like his first wife. It's the way some of these ranchers do things around here. They come from generations of cowboys, hard-bitten tough men. They do business and politics like they're a gang of gunfighters."

"Texas reminds me of my home in that way. Only a few men have the land and everyone else…we live homeless and they get more business with the government, they pay the officials...like in Mexico, the old Spanish way."

"You ever hear the story how Jorg's family bought this ranch a long time ago?"

"No," said Marta.

"Jorg's great grandfather captured the notorious outlaw John Wesley Hardin after a shooting aboard a train in Florida. The government granted him a four thousand dollar reward…a fortune back then. He bought the first fifty thousand acre plot from the owners of an old Spanish land grant and it's almost doubled in size since."

"Interesting," she said, "like the cowboys, wild west, and gunfights."

"I made a mistake. He's rotten," said Kate.

"Why did you marrying him?"

"Why did you marry your husband? You wanted a home, right?"

"So, you divorce and get the house or money."

"I divorce, he won't give me a dime."

"You be nice to him, maybe he give you a lot of money and keep you as a friend, a mistress."

"You mean one of many girlfriends? He pays them cheap, maybe a new car and nice dinners in exchange for what he wants. Over sixty now…he's not going to change, an old dog set in his ways. And at almost thirty, I'm back out at The Rancheros Lounge shaking my assets with three maybe four more good years at the high-paying joints, then I wind up in the slut bars turning tricks for tips. Jorg used to love it when I'd dress up like a cowboy for him, crack a bull whip out here on the patio and strip down to just the dirty leather leggings and the Stetson hat. He'd run around the pool chasing after his cowgirl."

"Uh-huh." Marta nodded her head.

She thought how it must be dancing naked, men watching, desiring. It was a sin...*un pecado*...that she could not commit, something she'd learned at church, not to arouse lust in men, but she didn't know where that rule was in the Bible. She learned a lot of rules—rules not to avoid having babies, though, she managed never to have any and didn't want any. In Nuevo León there were always hundreds of new babies every year and little food.

"You don't want to stay with him," Marta said finally after a pause, "but you want a home. I am like you in this way. I not care to stay with my husband but I wanted a home."

Kate picked up the crystal pitcher and poured another round of drinks. She dragged on her cigarette and blew smoke into the silent evening, stars glistening in the broad open sky.

Marta sipped her drink, watching the brunette and thinking she was on the edge of telling her some secret. Finally she blurted out, "What if something terrible happen to your dear Jorg?" Then she fell silent, sipped her drink, waiting for a reaction…maybe a stupid thing to say.

Kate grinned and said, "How did it turn out for your husband? How'd you feel? I mean after."

"I am religious and go to church," Marta explained, "to pray for him, so I'm sure he's resting in a much better place where he have no anger, more peaceful where he not need to beat me. So, is better dis way."

"Yes, it's better. He went to a better place," Kate said then paused, dragged on her glowing Silvest Sylvia, ashes growing long at the tip, blew white smoke against the darkness. "How much would a terrible accident cost?"

"Forty thousand cash and you don't think about it. Is *facil*...easy," said Marta immediately, "...and ten thousand cash for me...I organize things for you. You'll see how simple, quiet things happen."

Kate stood up, cigarette between her fingers, paced a few steps next to the swimming pool. "It's like a prison here. I can't take this anymore...some way to make it easier." She flicked the Silvest Sylvia butt into the cactus garden.

"No talk about it," said Marta. "Cash first. You not talk about it. No cash, nothing happen."

"I don't have that much cash and I can't withdraw money like that," Kate said, glancing at Marta. She paused, then pointed her finger in the air as if to say wait one minute. She went into the house and a couple minutes later came back with a small leather purse and handed it to Marta. "Forty...all I have."

"*Hecho*," said Marta, fingering through the purse.

"What guarantees do I have with you?"

"An accident…within seven days or I give you back the purse," she said, holding up her glass to seal the agreement in a ceremonial toast.

Three days passed. Kate pranced around the house restless and said to Marta, "Tomorrow's Wednesday. How about we drive up to San Antonio again, go to that spa, get a pampering?"

They stayed at the spa for hours—pedicure, manicure, facial, massage, steam room, hairstyling, sponge bath…. The brunette put it on her credit card. They decided to take in a romantic movie, the one about the bachelor President of the United States who fell in love with an ordinary French girl. During the afternoon matinee, they were practically alone in the cinema. They sat close together and enjoyed each other's caresses.

During the drive back to the ranch, they listened to a Lucinda Williams CD. Driving south on 77, Kate shared a joint with Marta, who sang and moved with the music. They laughed and toked away while the wind blew through the half opened windows in the black Lincoln Continental.

They stopped for an hour at the Long Horn Restaurant outside Corpus Christi. After lobster salads and drinks, they rolled deeper into Kleberg County, and then took King Road to the ranch. From a half mile away, they noticed the flashing lights. Closer now they could see it was the Kleberg County Sheriff cars.

The head sheriff walked up to Mrs. Bein and explained that her husband was at Corpus Christi Emergency but arrived dead. Marta stood nearby and took in the whole story. The ranch workers noticed the man floating in the pool and reported the accident early afternoon. As far as the sheriff and coroner saw it, Mr. Bein slipped, hit the back of his head on the edge of the pool. Case closed.

#

A day after the funeral, Kate drove back to the ranch to pickup the last of her possessions. Marta rode along with her. The brunette explained things to her. Contingent on Mr. Bein's death, the prenuptial agreement granted Kate with a generous life insurance claim and the condo in Houston. Marta waited in Kate's Lincoln Continental while she dashed into the ranch house. When Kate finished loading the car with her last bag, the three ranch hands rode up offering her a ride on one of their mounts for old times' sake. They let out a chuckle as if sharing some inside joke.

Kate sat behind the wheel next to Marta who told them, "*Callense*."

Odd how quickly the men fell silent.

"No, thank you." Kate declined their offer. "It'd probably feel liberating but I didn't know how to ride." She shook her head as she and Marta rolled away down the long gravel road.

Fog in Berkeley

Summer was coming on and there was a sultry feel in the weather. The San Francisco Bay fumed in thick fog rolling up over the Oakland docks and curling on up the Berkeley hills, making everyone feel a little isolated and damp.

Friday night in Berkeley, Rodevik had nowhere to go, no one to meet. He sat down at the bar in McMurphy's and sipped an Irish coffee. After the second one, he ordered an Irish whiskey straight up as was his routine for the last year. He cocked his butt to one side of the bar stool, his feet wedged between the brass foot rest and the bottom of the bar at the stone floor, just so he could stay alert. He waited. Maybe one of his drinking buddies would show up. Maybe one of the gals who worked at the nearby massage parlor would come in. He could talk for a while, warming up to a visit for an exotic massage, sensual Swedish style. Some biker guys were playing eight-ball at the tables in the back. He ignored them, figuring they were nothing but trouble.

"Slow night," he said to the bartender who wiped the freshly washed glasses dry with a towel.

"Aw, a little early yet," said the bartender, squinting at the front door, "folks get thirsty right about now."

Rodevik sat, sipped, and pondered the universe for a moment. What law of physics was it that did not allow him to lift his barstool while he sat on it with his feet off the ground? How is jacking-off any different from sex with a woman? His thoughts moved quickly to the subject preoccupying him. Then how could a person really get to know himself? Is that any more possible than an alarm clock knows itself? What law of physics pertained to self-knowledge? Physics is the key. He could break through, make a discovery, become recognized. Women would come to him. He had been studying at UC Berkeley for a couple years but almost every two months changed his major. Losing patience with his own thoughts, he set his feet flat on the floor and twisted around to look at the burly bikers playing pool guzzling down beers.

He fidgeted with a string he'd picked up from the bar. It held a key to the restroom, and a bottle opener, most likely to help the bartender not lose the key. The string also held a couple of beads, smaller than pool balls but imitating them in color and texture.

Rodevik took the string, brought it around the back of his hand, and over the palm where he held the two balls, wove the string between his third and fourth fingers so that the key and bottle opener pulled tight against the side of his hand at the little finger now closed in a fist around the balls.

He watched the hefty bikers, their leather jackets, some lame patch on their backs saying, "Mongoloids," or "Mongols," or some such damn thing that he could barely make out in the shadowy, smoke-filled bar. In any case, they were swackoed on beer and whiskey, staggering, slurring their words. It was enough to make a fair brawl.

His chronic anxiety grew tight across his chest and the muscles in his back and legs. He felt the string go slack so he undid it from his hand and started over, pulling the string tighter and over at one of the two pool tables, one of the bikers shot him a glance, like some cannon ball across his bow. What is he looking at? Son of a bitch. Is he looking at my face? Bastards are laughing, saying something about acne. By now he had the string tight on his hand again but tighter this time and he called out, "The fuck you lookin' at?"

Bikers in dark dives carried their own hot charge. The leather jackets, the patch, 'colors,' on their backs emitted an intimidating aura.

Rodevik stared the man down, the one who'd laughed and made a remark, the heavy set guy. At closer inspection, the man's hair and beard were graying. His eyes and cheeks sagged probably from drug and alcohol abuse.

He figured he had one advantage—he didn't care. He'd given this a little thought. Death might just be one of the most underrated events, maybe even a solution—a logical conclusion to some spiritual argument about ultimate faith. Besides, he was in his early twenties, going up against a gang of old, tough farts might be as exhilarating as some rodeo bull ride he'd always dreamed of as a rite of passage into manhood. What the hell. He stood up from his bar stool in a defiant gesture while still focused on the old biker's eyes, blood shot from the whiskey.

In the first go-round, the mean son-of-a-bitch walked up to him and said, “You got a foul mouth.”

Redevik decked him flat out, first punch. It changed all perspective, landing his fist, buttressed with the balls, smack on the man’s temple. When the bastard fell down, he hit his head on a wooden chair. He struggled for a minute in vain, squatted, twisted in spasms, and finally passed out.

That’s when two more guys lurched at him from across the room.

He threw another punch at one of the two, the weight and size of the balls tight in his fist equalized the odds. His fist struck square across the attacker’s nose just below the eye.

The gangster reeled back on his heels and stumbled, blood draining from his smashed cartilage, and fell on his back, banging his head on the floor.

Rodevik counted on luck, but when he woke up, he had lost all sense of time. At first it startled him that he was still alive. It was the bartender who had to explain to him that the other guy had broken a cue stick across the back of his head. That explained why his hair dripped with blood and the thumping pain in his head took precedence over the dullness of his otherwise ongoing morass.

"I called the cops and pulled out my baseball bat," said the bartender. "I'll be damned if somebody gets beat to death in my place. You should know better than to mess with them. They got out in a hurry when they heard me on the phone with the cops."

When Rodevik felt the knot on his head, he knew it had been a hairline step between this world and the great beyond. What the hell, he was still here and with a skull like someone had emptied it out and slipped one of the pool balls in it to bounce around for the sharp throbbing pain. He had no health insurance, so seeing a doctor was out of the question. What's the point anyway?

"I gotta go," he said, mouth bloody from a split lip, spitting. He managed to regain his feet and staggered out of the bar before the police arrived.

Back at his student dormitory, with dark hair as thick and heavy as a mop, Rodevik spent half an hour washing the blood out. He poured a pint of oxygen-peroxide over the gash in his scalp and suspected it might need a stitch or two, but the bleeding stopped. Without realizing for most of his life, he was more than good-looking when cleaned-up in fresh clothes, a white shirt and jeans, but he could hardly overlook the acne that speckled his face.

Six foot four, fidgeting, tapping, head-bobbing, he emanated edgy nerves. A virgin until almost twenty—unlike any of this school buddies—his attempts at losing that condition failed every time and as far as his desperation carried him, seemed to continue on and on until he finally discovered a massage parlor in Berkeley. He uncovered an outlet, and there was always open access so long as he had a few bucks in his pocket, though it was the tall fashion models he mounted in the privacy of his imagination.

Starting with his mother, things always seemed to go bad with women, she would often scold him when he first turned adolescent, punishing him when he stayed suspiciously long in the shower or looked too eagerly at the lingerie sections in the ladies clothing catalogue. From his perspective his mother always needled him for every little thing. Instead of the tender love he craved without even realizing it at the time, often received scorn, the domineering kind, that overbearing authority that crushed his budding self. And his father was a tough guy from the Nebraska farms, roughed up in combat against the Germans.

A week later Rodevik found himself sitting at the same barstool at McMuphy's on University Avenue. Friday night packed in every lonely heart searching for a score. This was the spring of his second year at UC Berkeley. Already twenty-two years old, he was failing most of his classes. Chin in hand, elbow braced at the bar, he drummed his fingers attempting to follow incoherent rap music and the yap of drunkards around him, when Lilli's long brown hair appeared in the corner of his eye and flowed over his nervous fingers.

She was his favorite of the masseuses he'd met in the course of his Arabian night adventures.

"You want to work this weekend?" She winked one of her half-dollar, green eyes and flashed her ultra-bright smile framed in thick luscious lips.

"Lilli," he said and pushed up a smile, trying to match hers, while painfully aware that his face rippled with blueberry style acne. Among his maddening blemishes, dark blond stubble added to his rough hue. Cigarette and pot smoke floated thickly in the scent of stale beer.

"Who's offering?" he asked, calculating how many dollars he had remaining in his pocket.

"Sheriff. He got word that you folded three Mongols. He sent me to make you an offer."

"Who's this Sheriff?"

"A guy owns a clubhouse down Dwight Way at the corner of San Pablo, down by the Oakland docks."

"What kind a club?"

"Place where guys wrestle, drink beer."

"What's the job?"

"Wrestling. He says you can make up to ten grand, one night, with talent like you."

"Never did that sort of thing. The rumble with those motorheads was an accident. It just happened. The guy charged on me. Some drunk maniac."

"Yeah, well, your story made it all the way to Sheriff somehow. Impressed him."

"My father taught me some boxin' and gave me a lesson or two, mostly the hard way."

“Don’t matter how,” she said. “You wanna make fast cash, you show up. Win or lose the fights, you still make some cash. Lilli gestured to his crotch and winked.

“You’ve seen it all. You been there?” he asked.

“No, never been there. Sheriff told me about it, invites me all the time, but I’ve never gone. Just guys who like motorcycles. You won’t get run down too much. Sheriff always has work. He can hook you up, if you want some regular job to pay rent. He’s the one helped me land the job massaging.”

“A career,” he said, grinning.

“Forty bucks an hour. I’m paying a mortgage on a condo overlooks the bay. Can claim as much, college boy? What? I ain’t in your league? That’s what you mean? University boy’n all.”

He sensed her frustration, maybe she wanted to make friends. He nodded.

She pulled a pencil from her small pink purse, drew a map, and left it next to his beer mug.

“Tomorrow night. Ten o’clock.” She held his eyes with hers for a second and walked off.

The good weather blew away eastward and the ocean currents carried rain and black clouds, darkening the night more than usual. A group of crotchscratchers stood outside in front of a dilapidated warehouse.

As if standing guard near their dozens and dozens of hawgs, several bikers milled around out in front of the warehouse. They were dressed in black leather jackets and blue jeans, as a standard uniform. Most of them were heavy-set dudes who probably grew up on Big Macs and Coca-Cola.

Rodevik rode up on his Honda 360 and parked it across the street from the collection of Harleys parked in perfect military formation as if a command kept the unit organized.

The prospect of money drew Rodevik to one of the worst areas in Oakland. He had seen plenty of motorcycle bums like these but didn't know them and considered them knuckheaded morons for no other reason but that they conformed to club ethics, like any churchgoing congregation. He figured if he could punch out a couple of Mongols by accident and gain a gash in the head, then he could damn well fight a couple of these goons and cash in.

With hardly a handshake, a skunky, skinny man in his forties greeted Rodevik without giving his name. Rodevik explained that Sheriff had invited him.

"Yeah. Good deal. Boxing night," said the man, "Big party. Grunge band. Gambling money." As the man led him into the warehouse, he spoke in broken phrases as if some electrical connections shorted out in his head.

Rodevik eyed the guy's face. His neck and ear displayed the sort of tribal scars he'd seen in pictures from Africa, except these had no artistic pattern or symmetry.

The man caught the stare and nodded, saying, "Noticed my cosmetics? In my youth, a knife fight, near here."

The man's face made Rodevik at ease for a moment, helping him to ignore his own skin. As they entered the clubhouse, Rodevik turned his head, watching a tall woman with a great figure, dressed in weird, skin tight nylon from neck to foot, walk into a room and close the door behind her.

The skunky man said, "How 'bout it? Ready for some fun?"

Rodevik noticed two men open a door, enter a side room, and close the door behind them. He asked, "What kind of fun?" He had a flash that there were women in those side rooms.

"Boxin'," said the guy. "What you come here for. Make some blood money."

Rodevik had considered boxing classes at the university as a way to relax from his studies, but he figured the physics classes needed all his attention, besides his father had been in the amateur circuit for a couple years after military service and taught him most all he knew. And he'd taken karate and wrestling though high school until budget cuts snipped those courses in his senior year.

His unnamed guide walked ahead of him and pointed to a large open hall. In the center Rodevik saw a plywood boxing ring raised up about two feet off the cement floor. Only a single slack rope fenced the ring.

Men huddled in several small groups. They all wore tattoos, indicating their loyalties, 'Hells Angels' or 'Bones' on their shoulders or as patches on a shirt or a jacket. They talked among themselves in hushed tones, probably negotiating their bets on the fighters like bookies do at horse races.

Rodevik spotted one or two of the fighters moving around, in and out of the boxing hall. To him they looked murderous, but then so did the Mongols at the bar the other night.

"You fight too?" Rodevik asked his guide.

"No more," he said, "gotta a future, me." And the man went on giving him advice about keeping up a guard, the jab, the spike, the hook, and so on.

The unnamed guide vanished as fast as another man appeared from nowhere, saying, "I'm Sheriff. You the guy belted those Mongols?"

"Rodevik." He held out his hand.

"They call me Sheriff, 'cause I was once a Deputy Sheriff, LA County. And 'cause I own this place." He waved his hands around the dank, slapdash warehouse.

"Hey, listen, Rodevik, I got you set up for the next fight. Just step into the ring. We'll see what you got."

"What about the money?"

"What money?"

"Lilli," said Rodevik, "she told me I get ten grand for fighting tonight."

"Yeah," said Sheriff, "you can. You go place your bets with the guy with the big silver earring. The more you bet, the more you make."

Rodevik looked across the hall at the bookie with the earring. Before he could turn around, Sheriff was gone.

He bet $1,000 on himself. The bookie demanded the cash up front. Rodevik negotiated. The bookie argued that if he lost, he'd have to take every fight Sheriff demanded that night. If he won this first fight, his cut would be two grand.

"Five grand," said Rodevik.

"Two," said the bookie.

"Four."

"Three," said Rodevik, "And I can use my feet."

"Done," said the bookie.

Rodevik waited in the ring, determined to make some money. He didn't like the terms of his employment. He certainly didn't want to fight according to Sheriff's whims. He stripped down to his undershorts, giving boxer shorts a new meaning. He warmed himself up, jumping around the ring which cracked and creaked with every move. He threw practice punches in the air, imagining how he would clobber his first opponent.

When the opponent stepped into the ring, it was clear that Sheriff wasn't placing bets on Rodevik. His opponent stood half-naked, dressed only in shorts, a good three inches taller, worst yet, his weight was at least sixty pounds more. Simple law of physics, something about two bodies of mass colliding and the larger one producing more energy and resistance.

Without pause or thought, Rodevik jumped in. His opponent didn't have time to tie one of his dangling shoe laces. Rodevik punched him in the belly with a right jab and hooked the giant's jaw with a left. It didn't stop the bearded goliath from punching him square in the chest. It threw Rodevik back with such a force that his kidneys hit the rope and he slipped off the platform and landed flat on his side in the filth covered cement floor.

The crowd cheered, revealing how everyone had placed their bets. The scam they ran on Rodevik was blatant and only enraged him to win. No sooner had he jumped back to the ring, than he kicked the giant with all the force of his leg straight at the back of the knee. The monster's legs folded and as he fell, Rodevik hooked him under the chin, partly punching his Adam's apple. When the weight hit the plywood, it collapsed into a hole the size of the man's butt where he busted through and slammed on the concrete floor, choking, gagging, and struggling for breath.

Sheriff raised Rodevik's hands as the undisputed victor. "You know what," said Sheriff, "you just might make a fighter."

Rodevik claimed his cash winnings, shoved the bills deep into a buttoned pocket, and sat, sipping water and pouring it over his sweating head. Leaning back against a cinder block wall, he replayed the fight in his mind, the feeling his life had jumped into a new dimension. His legs shook from an adrenaline rush that made euphoria flow through him like new blood.

He remembered then back in some lost past how his father took a couple days off work for the first and only time they had an extended weekend for the whole family to go to the lake. He loved the water. His dad gave him his first real boxing lessons, one of the rare moments when his father paid any attention to him.

Some biker came up and shook him by the collarbone and rattled him back to the present. The stranger handed him a bottle. It burned like kerosene, flaming all the way down his throat and exploding in his gut.

He leveled his eyes to see some other biker walking around sipping some of the same bourbon, a wet erection still standing strong out of his zipper. A woman stood up from a couch, adjusting a tight fitting leather skirt that had been pushed up above her waist.

He sipped a little more of the bourbon and as he tilted his head back to swallow and spotted a U.S. Marine Corps flag on a wall. Over by the couch two women started fighting. One of them was the woman who'd just pulled her skirt back into place not a minute ago. They went at it, kicking crotches, pulling hair, and punching. A few men howled and formed an eager audience. They were probably fighting over the man who'd just waxed his wick.

American violence was on display here at its best, free and wild. The military stockade country, the only one with its televised professional wrestling circus and its very own Military Channel, the one with history's largest military budget and still couldn't seize the oil from a country smaller than the state of Texas in a preemptive blitzkrieg. Violence for the sake of gain, money, booty, pussy—that was exactly why Rodevik showed up here. He wiped the sweat off his brow, his adrenaline rush wearing down. The only thing closest to water now were the cans of beer sold from a beat-up soda machine that stood near the couch where the women had just finished their brawl and disappeared into dark rooms. He bought a can of Bud Light as he noticed the rank smell of a toilet pipe. He then saw how a sewer line ran down a wall from the second floor above, leaking its filth onto the floor from a crack.

A biker sat next to him on the couch while he drank his Bud. The man introduced himself as Blade. Long greasy blond hair strung over is broad shoulders, held together by a star-spangled bandana in red, white, and blue. A 'Bones' patch was stitched on his black leather jacket. His hands were thick, three of his finger nails were bruised black and barely attached from the knocks—signs of a real boxer.

Blade congratulated him on his win in the ring and said, "You like the clubhouse?"

"Luxurious palace."

"Hey, Sheriff owns this place, man, he was a real Sheriff once. He bought this place, like the American Dream. You know, pride in home ownership. He served in Afghanistan and then in Iraq, a Marine, fighting man. When he come back, the county told him his job was gone, that he'd been away too damn long. Someone else took it. He found out there's law about that, says they can't do that, and, and Sheriff, he won somethin' like five hundred grand and he bought this place. It's our home, needs a little work, maintenance, cleaning, you know."

"Yeah," said Rodevik, pointing with his finger. "Leaking sewer line."

"Hey," said Blade, "we're taking care a that. It's prospects' job. They keep the place clean, maintain it. You do that for a year, you're allowed in with a full patch, part of family. But you gotta do whatever a member asks you. Wash a bike. Mop the floor. Fix a pipe.

"Looks like your prospects are on top of their job," he said.

"Most of all, you gotta fight at all the parties," said Blade.

"Sounds like a real good deal." He crushed the beer can in his hand and dropped it on the floor. "Work as a slave for a year and join a nuthouse."

"Man," said Blade, "you got some fight in you. You'd make a good prospect. What Sheriff wants."

"A career move."

"There's a lot of benes," said Blade.

He considered the proposition. "I don't think so," he said in his side-of-the-mouth voice, and let out a beer belch.

"You don't get it, man," said Blade. "Women dig this. Pussy galore. It's not the skanky ones either. I get laid by the creamy ones, well-heeled attorneys, models, smart business divas. They dig this dark, clammy palace where they can sneak away from the high roller pricks and get it raw and hardcore. They like dabbling in the far side, living a secret life. Helps them to balance out, working in them skyscraping offices where they can't find any men with huevos. But there are rules. You wanna join up, you can't screw a member's chick for the first year. You can't do hard drugs, and you have to carry a cell-phone, be on call always to help out in a pinch. And that piece a shit Honda I seen you park across the street, you can send that to the Salvation Army. We can fix you up with a real bike. Dignity, man. What a real bike is."

"I can see that," said Rodevik, "but your club, don't make sense. I study at the university, physics. I'll get a real job, good money. That's dignity. Not this." He waved his hand toward the filth dripping from the cracked sewer line and pulled another one-dollar beer from the soda machine, painted red with Coca-Cola written in big white flowing letters.

"We're a small club, a family. Most a us're former Marines, Recon guys, couple a mechanics, a guy with a Ph. D. teaches college, a veterinarian. You don't wanna join, fine. Fuck it. Think it over though. There's also a beat-down before you get your patch."

"A beat-down, huh?" He asked.

"We strip you naked and knock the shit outta ya. Our way to enlighten you."

"Enlightenment?" He sat on the arm of the couch, opened his beer, and let his attention focus on a woman, dressed in a tight yoga outfit, walking by with two members following her like a couple of puppies, one of them howling, eying her tight, yoga slim body.

"Damn right," said Blade, "you learn the elemental of being a man in this fucked up world. You grow up, most of us come from fucked up families, some cheap cookie-cutter urban sprawl, riding our little banana-seat bicycles down to the levee. People out there making babies by the bushel, thinking it's their ticket to happiness or like it's some god-damn church rule."

Wondering what the hell he was doing sittin' there wasting his time with this knuckleheaded Blade. It made Rodevik keenly aware that he had hardly the skill and patience for friendship, least of all fraternity, and less for affection, kept himself shielded from love, though behind his armor, when later it did come down on him, it trapped him and swallowed him up. He was done, couldn't go back home and he remained an outsider at the university. He painfully admitted to himself just then how he didn't fit in and he was failing, though trying, sweating blood to get an education, become the vague idea he had of a professional. But all that seemed a million miles away. No one in his family, hardly anyone he knew, had gone to college. It left him clueless as to how to behave, what to do.

"You agree to become a prospect," said Blade, "let me know. Sheriff wants to add a smart guy or two. It's a family, fraternity of social rebellion here. We're free because we remain elemental, ourselves, freed from living in the old mold." Blade hadn't finished his thought when a tall brunette walked up and sat on his lap.

Rodevik took her for one of the frustrated attorneys from the financial district that Blade had mentioned.

"Hi Bladie boy," said the lady, "who's your friend?" Her long legs awkwardly brushed against Rodevik's as he sat higher on the couch's arm. Her high-heels fell off her feet and rolled across his lap and on to the floor. He sat motionless, affecting the tough, jaded look. A voice down the hall boomed out calling Blade. It sounded like Sheriff.

Blade slipped out from under the elegant woman, stood up, and quickly disappeared into the dark hall in the direction of the shouts for him. Without Blade to prop her up, the woman sank deeper into the couch. Her legs higher above her. She rested her bare feet on Rodevik's thighs.

"You Blade's buddy?" She asked, and bent one of her knees leaving just enough peeking space for his curiosity.

He noticed the sheer, lace panties that hardly covered her precious treasures and said, "No, we just met."

"I saw you fight. You have a lot of energy and, and stamina." She smiled. "Oh, my name's Fay. She crossed her legs to lean forward and shake his hand. In that movement, her short skirt rolled up her thighs, exposing a lot more than peeking space.

Rodevik eyed her charms and smiled with a handshake. And in one smooth movement, she held his hand and pulled him down into the couch next to her. She rolled to her side and wrapped a leg over his as he abandoned himself next to her.

By the following Thursday, Rodevik found himself sitting at a small table in the dark corner of McMurphy's. Lilli showed up with a thickly rolled joint and they shared the moment. He bought the beers to quench the cotton mouth thirst of cannabis. He'd tried and tried to study, but he couldn't focus with the wild clubhouse woman on his mind. He was happy Lilli came. She was beginning to seem more like love compared to the new, unimaginable lust at the clubhouse. He could still smell the musky scent of the lawyer lady, an alpha female, whose name he didn't remember, but whose primordial antics on the dirty couch he'd never forget.

"You and me, we're like buddies, don't you think?" Lilli said with eyes red from the pot, black pupils dilated, pushing back her green irises to the white edges.

"I guess so," he said, "I'm happy you're here. You saved my butt. I was running out of money."

"I heard you did good at the Bones' clubhouse."

"You didn't show up there."

"No," she said, "Never seemed like my kind of place."

"How so?" He asked.

"Too wild for me. A lot of loose women, drugs, violence. Maniac parties. I'm not that type."

"Really," he said, "you being a masseuse and all. I figured you—"

"You got the wrong impression, dude. I might wank you off when you're on the table. But I do that 'cause I thought you were nice. A lot a the guys who come in for a massage have awful attitudes. But the job pays the bills."

"Yeah, I thought otherwise, that maybe you were doing all your clients."

"You thought wrong. Let's not talk about it, okay?" She sipped her beer and then said, "Just because I do you a little pleasure, you think I'm some kind a hooker, huh?"

"Didn't say that. I just—"

"Yeah, well whatever. Stupid."

"No," he said. "Hey, let's be friends, nice. I like you."

"Why?"

"You've been nice with me. But I'm not such a nice guy, you know? I can't keep a girlfriend more than twenty minutes after."

"After what?" She asked.

"You know."

After a silent pause, she said. "That was good pot. Truth serum. You never talked with me like that before."

"What? Like what?"

"You never tell me your feelings. Like you don't have any or don't know them."

"Yeah. I like you."

"Good start," she said and slid across the booth seat closer to him.

"My parents think I'm studying hard. They'd never dream I'm smoking dope and hanging out like this. Back home in Modesto, everybody thinks of me as some kind of uptight narc."

"You *are* uptight," she said.

"So what? And you? What're you then?"

They both sipped their beers and looked out the window as the sun fell and the city lights grew stronger. He managed to put his arm around her and give her several warm, French kisses. He wanted to run to home base right there in the dark corner of McMurphy's, but she stood up when he knew she was warming up, and gave some lame reason why she had to run.

He lay down in the grassy area next to the marina and watched the sailboats that Sunday. By afternoon, his thoughts roamed around the notion how rich people got richer and poor people just got kids. Nothing made sense to him. He didn't know how to make it in school. His father worked all day and came home with hands black from the grease of the big trucks and earth moving equipment. He could hardly understand how to cross the invisible line between the clean, well paid white collars driving Porches or sailing in the bay and the sweaty, blue collars. He'd never make it, useless to try. Stupid to even believe he could cross the great divide, might as well swim across the bay. He had no control of his thoughts and they sank him to the bottom of the waters. Considering suicide, he made several elaborate schemes and settled on the one that seemed most practical. Take a rubber raft, paddle out to the middle of the bay with his feet tied to the anchor, use a 9mm Glock to shoot holes in the raft, and then shoot a hole in his head.

Theory M—something he learned in physics about parallel universes in the eleventh dimension. His soul would simply slip through to one of those other places. And Lilli—he would ask her to go with him. So damned alone, he wasn't good enough for her. She won't go with him. He would call his mom first. One last talk and then he'd do it. He tried everything, chemistry, lab assistant, spectrometry. Nothing panned out. He couldn't finish anything. At times he couldn't believe his father was really his. How could he possibly be born into a blue collar family? There must be some mistake. Other times he wondered how he might cross over, succeed.

Rodevik's parents had a small stucco house in Modesto, the center of the San Joaquin Valley. His mother, a housewife, had five kids and husband to manage. He was the oldest of the litter, the first to go to college and since his experience in higher education had turned into calamity, his parents didn't encourage his younger sisters and brothers. He knew it wasn't working out. He walked down the street toward McMurphy's, searching for a solution and found a phone booth.

When he called his mother and told her the latest news in his career plans, she went through the roof.

"What's this idea?" said his mother. "Just because your father did a little boxing doesn't mean you make a career of it. Your father sweats out under the sun, working his fingers raw, fixing trucks so you can get an education. Now you wanna be a boxer? By god, you go ahead and ruin your life. We did everything we could to give you opportunities. You wanna throw it all away, fine."

"I'm already making money boxing," he said. "You don't send me money to go to school, so there's no way I can do it."

"You do this just to spite your father," she said. "You're a hateful brat. You're not getting help from us for this."

"I didn't ask for it," he said, standing in a phone booth outside McMurphy's. "I'don't need it."

"You need plenty of help. You know darn well that boxing's for fools, no way to make a living."

"It's done," he said. "I'm already making my living this way." He couldn't go back now. He had found his vocation.

"You cause your father nothing but worry, Dev. You're a pain. As stubborn as he is. You go on then. Do what you want. I can't stop a train wreck. But I won't pickup the pieces afterward. You take after him."

Bitch. He thought but kept it to himself. He wanted to tell her to stop repeating the same old crap.

"Don't call me Dev," he said. "Least you could do is use the name you gave me." He smashed the receiver on the hook, banged the phone booth door open, and walked into McMurphy's for a beer.

He had called Lilli to reserve a time for massage but she didn't answer. He left her a message about meeting at McMurphy's.

As he sat sipping a beer, hoping she would arrive, the thought of attending some boxing school crossed his mind. He'd had enough of school.

The end of spring term had come, leaving him behind to dry out in the sun. He'd failed one of his classes and barely passed the others. He sat there in the dark corner of the pub watching for Lilli and worried that maybe a Mongol or two might show up again. The money was running out after three weeks since his win at the clubhouse. It was surprising how no Mongols ever came back for revenge. "Scared them all away," he said to himself with a cocky tone.

As the school year ended he hung on to the last days of life in the student dormitory. He'd been hanging out at the gyms on University Avenue, trying to negotiate a job—even if it meant janitor—so he could absorb more tips about boxing. One of the managers at Gold's offered him minimum wages and a bunk in the janitor's room. He took every offer to spar with the lawyers and office workers who came in looking for the thrill. He often fought off the urge to give one of them a real punch. Instead he pretended to spar at their rate, throwing soft punches with the big, cushy gloves which he never wore at the clubhouse. It was all playful appearances to bring money into the gym. Those guys knew as much about real fighting as they might about repairing a Mac truck.

He took up reading Nietzsche, considered it himself an Uebermensch, and often quoted Zarathustra to himself. "Every church is a stone on the grave of a god-man: it does not want him to rise up again under any circumstances." He took it seriously and thought of it as his religion, as good as any other.

"Where is Lilli," he said to himself, and ordered another beer.

At the gym he'd been taking every opportunity to spar and train when it was free and nagged the manager to pay him to babysit the dough-boy office workers. He lived on junk food and dove into this life of nicks and bruises with its violence and blood. The woman on the couch in the clubhouse lay naked in the back of his mind like some permanent wall paper decorating his imagination.

He felt alive only when he sparred in the gym's ring and learned some new boxing tricks from the hoity-toity personal trainers who'd attained black belts in martial arts. He craved a real fight and looked forward to another round at the clubhouse. It lit a fire in his gut to think of it, igniting a rush to this otherwise unbearable existence. He went at it like a lone wolf after fresh meat, raw and red.

"I was beginning to think you were too pure to show up here," said Rodevik watching Lilli pace straight to his shadowy table, wearing a short skirt, black leotards, and a loose shirt.

"Still chewing on our last meeting, huh?" She pushed back her thick hair and flashed her perfectly whitened teeth.

“Can’t help it. Wake up in the morning, you’re in my thoughts.”

“That’s sweet talking,” she said, sitting in the booth next to him. “Watch out, it’ll get you in trouble.”

“Good. How about a beer?”

“Sure. So you still in school?”

“Summer break. I got a little job at Gold’s Gym as a personal trainer for the half-wit office workers. I’m thinking of going back to the Bones’ clubhouse, make more money boxing.”

“Feeling your lucky streak?”

“I need to make money,” he said, “so far it’s the quickest way. You and me, I guess we both go after the easy money.”

The waiter set two beer mugs on their table. Lilli lifted hers and toasted, “Here’s to easy money.”

They clicked their mugs together and sipped. “Getting in that boxing ring is not so easy, though, is it?” She asked.

“Sometimes I think it’s the least of it,” he said, his fingers fidgeting with his beer mug.

"Doing massage isn't as easy as you think. Some of the men come in looking for something else. But a good massage can be as good as any sex."

"Really?" He asked. "Never thought of it that way. Anyone ever give you a massage?" He slid closer to her, rubbing her back.

"Yes," she said, "really. You know something? You probably take life too much like it's real. You have any spirituality about you?" She relaxed, soaking up the massage.

He felt the small of her back, let his hand knead the muscles on the sides of her spine and around her neck.

She put her hand on the back of his neck, massaging his shoulders, and in one smooth pull, brought him near to her and kissed him on the lips.

This ignited all sorts of bells and lights, mostly green "go" signals in his mind. He passed his hand around her waist and up to grope her breast.

"Hey," she whispered and pulled back from the entangled limbs. "Cool your rockets. Not here."

"Where then?" He asked.

"Come to my place?" She said.

"I'm going to the clubhouse tonight, make money."

"I have to work late anyway," she said. "Come later."

"Fine."

They sipped beers and gazed into each other's eyes, smiling, losing all sense of time.

"I'm thinking of joining up," he said.

"What? The Army?"

"No," he said. "The Bones."

She paused and looked around the bar, the pool tables, the dart boards, and the calendar with half-naked beautiful women on the June page. "I'd think you got more sense than joining up with a gang of n'er do-wells. What about school?"

"It's summer…I gotta do something. He twirled his beer mug, sloshing its foam over the brim.

"You hear what happened to the Mongols?" She asked.

"No."

"The ATF busted them in five states all at the same time. They had three undercover officers collecting evidence for three years. They were cooking up and selling meth. They're finished now."

"That explains why none of them shows up here anymore."

"I just hope the Bones isn't into anything like that."

"I doubt it," he said.

"I gotta go," she said, picking up her purse, pulling her shirt and skirt back into place.

"I'll see you tonight," he said bobbing his head.

She turned and waved as she walked out.

Before the sun went down, Rodevik was shifting his motorcycle into fourth gear, passing buildings with the wind whipping through is hair, speeding down San Pablo Avenue toward the clubhouse. He had gotten a taste of the place and wanted more. His imagination saw women darting in and out of dark rooms where secret ceremonies were being performed. He yearned to know this hidden world, to be part of it. He had sensed the exhilaration of the shadow between life and death like an alternative reality, only more real than the routine out in the city lights, the emerald skyscrapers sparkling from across the bay, the pyramid, the embarcadero, the financial district's bank penetrating the clouds. It appeared so beautiful and, at the same time, standing on fraud.

The kids straight out of college who sell their dreams out to a promise of fast money in the brokerage houses or in the banks counseling the average consumer on how to invest for a retirement that never comes because the mutual funds and mortgages are all used as chips in an international poker game for higher profits.

After parking his beat-up Honda out of sight, he stood catching a breath of air before entering the dank warehouse. He came across one of the lower club members who introduced himself as Skin. He was bleeding from a gash above his eye, beat in a fight not ten minutes ago, still sweating and on the tail end of an adrenaline high, crashing from the rush, and now showing the pain in his head and the broken pride.

"I lost, man, lost a fight. What the hell," he said. "One night I'm winning and flying light as the angels, next night I'm fucked. Thirty-six years old and still busting heads."

To Rodevik, Skin looked almost like a kid despite his age. Nursing his wound, he revealed an accent, a talk like someone who'd grown up in middle America, trying to escape the rotting urban life in Oakland.

Blood trickling from a split lip, he rolled a reefer with Ziggy papers and lit it saying, "Gotta calm my nerves." He puffed it and passed it to Rodevik who took a drag.

He blew smoke, passed the joint back to Skin. They both looked over Oakland's decaying neighborhoods and out across the bay to the City. A vague intuition hit him how he was trying to stand up to this, the old puritan dog-eat-dog American way, learning how to adopt to it somehow, to eat it up fearlessly, toughen up his nerves and senses against it. The fight was somehow part of digesting it, taking it all in, embodying the rugged American survival with few rules, except elusive market forces.

Skin finished the reefer before Rodevik could turn around and look for another toke.

"I come from the Central Valley, man, you know." Skin said, revealing just how stoned the pot made him by his slow annunciation of words. "I lived downtown, not far from the port, always been looking at docks, worn down warehouses, closed down canneries, tall grain silos."

By this time another low level member approached, visibly drawn in by the aroma of fine, top buds burning and said, "Man, you talking about that White Supremist bull you picked up in—where was it? Modesto, right?" The stranger didn't bother to introduce himself, lit a cigarette when he discovered the reefer was finished, and tapped Rodevik on the shoulder to call his attention and said, "You gotta watch out about this dude, man, always spouting off about family values, and the Christian cause."

Skin shook his head in denial.

"He's a fuckin' Christian. Hey, he's all for this war in Iraq, wants them Arabs dead. He's married to a big legged blond, knocked her up. Only woman he ever pokes."

"Shut the fuck up, Dopper," said Skin. "That's my business. She's a good Christian girl, graduated from college too. You wouldn't know good when it bit you in the face." He pushed a wad of chew between his lips, making him slur when he said, "You're jealous you don't have a woman warming up your bed every night with some hot suckie. That's family dude, and I'm proud to be a Christian too."

The three men walked to the clubhouse entrance where a biker sat on the cement porch, holding down a Bull dog. Another biker held the dog's testicles tight against the scrotum, which he quickly sliced open with a razor blade and yanked them out with his fingers.

"That dog's been humping everybody's leg around here, so Sam, he's a veterinarian, he fixed it," said Dopper as he followed Skin and Rodevik into the clubhouse.

"That's Bull on the end there," said Dopper, pointing to the long table where several members were placing bets on their cards. Goddamn bikers all they talk about is their bikes like they was women. 'Oh, she's sweet, holds tight on the throttle, sucks the wind outta ya.'"

"They don't know bikes from girls, handlebars from tits," said Skin.

"You sit at that table," said Dopper, "you lose your shirt."

"I come here to fight," said Rodevik as he reached the poker table where one of the players pulled out a chair for him to join in. "I need to make money, not gamble it."

"Like fighting's a sure thing, huh?" One of the bikers said.

Rodevik hadn't seen this part of the clubhouse, reserved mostly for card games with its long, heavy wooden table that looked like somebody had hauled out of the bay, remnants of a pirate's shipwreck. Ashtrays piled with burned out, stale cigar stubs served as centerpieces. The walls were completely windowless and neon signs were hung as decorations. A neon 'Johnnie Walker' sign sparkled like an off-season Christmas tree. A couple of vintage 'Olympia Beer' signs buzzed on another wall, bright blue light animating Tumwater, Washington's river.

Rodevik stood next to the chair offered to him and said, "Surer than poker." He looked at the card players but didn't know any of them although he recognized some faces from his last visit. He'd heard that the Bones club comprised of less than thirty members. He noticed a few bikers at the table, wearing Hell's Angels colors on their jackets, big men, most of them showing receding hairlines, others with bandanas or long hair.

Rodevik recognized that he could get seriously drunk and lose money if he sat at the table. He picked up the faint smells of the half-puffed cigars lying dead or smoldering in the ashtrays, the stale beer, and the broken sewer line.

Dopper sat down next to a couple of Hell's Angels and anted up for the next deal of cards, and said, "Don't let Skin sit here, he'll chew your ear about how a wife heats up his bed."

Skin sat down wedged in next to Bull at the end of the table.

The beer cans and cigars came and went. Rodevik finally sat down and held cards but practically never placed a bet. In a while Bull started up talking about how he was once married and the regularity of conjugal pleasures. Then one of the Hell's Angels mumbled something about boredom and prison.

Skin went off on a rant about how he was soon to be a father. He waved his hands, crying a little about how he wanted to be a good father and bumped the row of his empty beer cans which fell clanging on the cement floor.

With five or six beers sloshing in his gut, Rodevik addressed the gamblers in turn. Even the grungy members, who'd wondered up to the table, looking for a seat, listened.

"You talk like girl scouts, all nostalgic about wife, kids, mom, and dad. But you're all here and this is home. How much time did you spend with your wife or kids when you lived with them? How much time did your marriages last? You never had the taste for it that's why you're here. Spend more time here than anywhere. No boss here to call you a retard. No wife telling you to hurry to work and take out the garbage."

One of the standing bikers started to say something but Bull stared him down.

"Here's to the club," said Rodevik and held up a beer can before he drank it all down without a breath. "Here's to it."

"They say we're misfits," said Bull, "but I don't understand what the hell it is we're supposed to fit into."

High as a kit and twice as drunk, Skin jumped up when Rodevik started again, saying, "I think this is family and I wanna join—" And he didn't know what he wanted to join except that Skin shouted something about God and the sacred union of man and wife and how gay marriage was an abomination, as he was wind-milling fists at Rodevik and clipped him on the nose while on a drunken fall, smashing face down on the oak table, among smoldering cigar stubs, scattering whiskey bottles, cards, and clanging beer cans as he passed out cold.

Blood dripping from his nose, Rodevik decided it was time to go home, except when he started his motorcycle he didn't quite know where home was anymore. He rode back up San Pedro Avenue, visualizing the image of the Great Dane getting fixed.

The Death of Ali

The Year 661 A.D.

As his horse paced along the dry riverbed, Salemad the Sufi raised his eyes just enough to watch what Muljam, the Khawarijite, was going to do next. Long before he had come around the bend, he had heard Muljam's mare snorting and whinnying.

Like a jackal, Muljam waited in the barren, silent terrain. There had been a time when the scoundrel would have fired a poisoned arrow at a rider on the caravan trail below him, especially when the rider was, in his view, an infidel and a friend of Ali Talib. Many times before, the man had killed for a fresh horse, a new robe, usually for more or better weapons. He suspected Muljam's reasons were always based on strict rules for judging who was or wasn't a Muslim. This time the Khawarijite had something on his mind. He hung his bow over his shoulder and urged his Arab mare down the sandy slope.

Salemad was certain Muljam had recognized him from afar. Muljam had known him ever since he had befriended Ali Talib, the fourth of the Rightly Guided Caliphs of the new Arabic religion of one God.

His thoughts ran through all this as he slouched forward in his saddle. He lowered his head against the sun's glare, turban low over his eyes. As the Khawarijite closed in, he raised his sights, as if he had just spied the approaching rider.

"*Allāhu Akbar*," Muljam said, using the Muslim greeting—God is great…though he mocked the words as if spitting them down into the hot sand.

Salemad, a mystic Sufi, didn't care one way or the other. He brushed at the strands of hair that frayed out from under his turban, and then fingered the battle scar that ran just below his brow. An ample, sweat-darkened robe protected his shoulders from the fierce sun, though his legs were mostly naked where the robe rumpled up against the saddle. His feet were wrapped in shoes of camel hide. A quiver of arrows hung across the front of his saddle.

"Now you greet me as a brother." He grinned at the Khawarijite and studied the man's narrow, long face. "Does this mean you want something?"

He had not seen Muljam in months, not since the Khawarij congregation had broken ties with Ali Talib, calling him a faithless infidel. The Khawarij…successors of the true faith…once the fervent supporters of Ali, now turned their backs on him, judging him as indecisive because he dealt with the Umayyad clan diplomatically rather than lead his army to annihilate them.

The Khawarij considered the Umayyads as unfaithful cheats who unfairly benefited from the third Caliph, Uthman. Rather than grant powerful political appointments to the Prophet Muhammad's family, the Hashimites, Uthman favored his own Umayyad clan. Uthman's rule was flawed by nepotism, giving important positions to his own family members, thinking it would only strengthen and centralize the new Islamic territories. That mistake cost Uthman his life when disgruntled soldiers killed him. It was only the beginning of brutal battles among the Muslims. In the streets men threw stones at Uthman's dead body during the funeral procession.

Salemad didn't know exactly who the assassin was, though Muljam remained at the top of his suspect list, especially since the man had left the territory, disappeared without a trace shortly after the attack. As a mystic, Salemad used psychic abilities that surpassed most any other Sufi. Wise men, elders of his Sufi groups, marveled at how well he could read a man's soul simply by studying his eyes and talking to him. Now Muljam was back, after the death of Uthman, and Salemad studied him, wondering why.

"You know and I know Ali Talib should never have made concessions with the Umayyads." The Khawarijite spoke in a deep, hoarse voice as if he'd gone off somewhere and howled out his prayers to the moon for many nights while smoking opium. "The entire *ummah*—" Muljam continued as if in the middle of some line of thought he'd been following long before Salemad showed up on the trail, "the community…suffers in the face of God for Ali's soft hand on an enemy of our faith. Ali is incapable of acting with the firmness of Muhammad and the other prophets…Moses…Abraham. Ali, your friend and you think only of your own skin. He acts in fear."

"And you…when did you begin to act out of charity?" Salemad asked.

"Those are my tribesmen in Mecca," Muljam said. "And now the Umayyads have taken control of Jerusalem too."

"No point arguing with you." Salemad shrugged. "Nothing I can do about Mecca. There's nothing I can do to help you. Maybe you will avoid problems if you go home, relax in the shade, maybe puff a little opium."

"Home? Where is that now, Salemad?"

"You need not ask. You know."

"In Mecca? You mean where the brother of Uthman, Muawiya, pushes us around? That is no way to live," said Muljam.

"Maybe if you put away your scimitar." He nodded to Muljam's sword handle attached at the front of his saddle.

"Yes, and we stand head bowed to Muawiya while his clan of Umayyads walks over us, taking away our livelihood on the trade roads through Mecca. Do as Ali Talib does…make concessions for those thugs."

"It is true that for a long time now I have befriended Ali." Salemad nodded. "You know that I am a Sufi…not inside the circles of the Muslim world. I only recognize Islam. And you know that I have advised Ali. He opens his heart to my words and I have made him aware of your grievances."

"Maybe you advise him wisely," said Muljam. "But what influence does a mystic have? None. Muhammad himself has shown us all that it is the sword that influences more than the poetry of the Koran. We merely follow his example in action. We turn our backs in protest to the behavior of the reigning caliph. We summon all true Muslims to join us in *jihad* for higher…purer standards."

Those words rang familiar to Salemad's ears and he said, "Muawiya uses violence against other Muslims, intimidating the Khawarijites in order to expand his own power. Muawiya accumulates a powerful army and waves his sword whenever the whim inspires him. I have explained this to Ali, who knows this and takes your grievances to heart, but he prefers to avoid conflict among Muslims. All Muslims know Ali as Muhammad's Tiger. And you of all people know this. He had fought as the fiercest Muslim at the Prophet's side."

Muljam nodded in recognition of this.

"I don't need to explain this to you," he insisted. "You were there."

The recent past ran through Salemad's thoughts as he paused, wondering how to turn Muljam's around. Years ago, when fighting broke out between the Muslims and the Meccan Quraish, Muhammad's own blood relatives, his clansmen. Ali had been on the forefront of the battlefield, proving his faith by fearless combat. The small Muslim army lined up facing the Meccan infidels at the Battle of Badr, the first of many battles to expand Islam. Both armies decided to send out their three boldest warriors to settle their differences in a three-on-three meleé to the death. Ali stepped forward as one of the Muslim warriors, and promptly defeated the Meccan champion Walid ibn Utba in single combat. Once the Muslim heroes defeated the Meccan pagans, a large-scale battle ensued. Ali led Muslims, who were outnumbered but much more organized. He slew the pagan nomads with his sword, which everyone called Zulfiqar—a large scimitar with a two-pronged, v-shaped point. His valor that day prompted Muhammad to grant his own daughter, Fatima, in marriage to Ali.

Although Salemad advocated peace, he admired Ali's bravery. Everyone had heard the legend about Ali's combat skill and courage. According to Shi'a tales, Ali once used Zulfiqar to cleave both a horse and its rider in half with one swing. His strong arm with Zulfiqar in hand would have cut a gaping hole in the earth if the Archangel Jibreel hadn't stayed Ali's hand. Everyone talked about how an archangel had to stop Ali from slicing a fissure in the firm ground. Yet Salemad recognized such a story as mere legend to encourage the soldiers to battle fearlessly.

For this very reason, it was strange that Ali cared for Muljam and his band of Khawarijites. They were extremists, calling both Ali and Uthman infidels, faithless leaders. Yes, he understood the Khawarijites' political maneuvering.

Calling Ali an unbeliever sounded ridiculous, but so be it. These Muslims believed in their one and only God, yet they killed each other for their vague understandings of the one way of this one God. It made little sense. Still he wondered what had made Muljam return here in Ali's new base territory at Kufa, on the banks of the

Euphrates. Perhaps he should leave the man be. He could work things out among his own Khawarijites. He had tried to advise Ali.

"Why would a man of your stature return now to Ali's base territory?" he asked Muljam. "Everyone knows you are one of the instigators of this costly war between your Khawarijites and the Umayyads. You and your friends caused the battle at Nahrawan…and Basra. If Ali's soldiers catch you, your fate might not be glorious."

Muljam said, "Then I will die and go to Paradise. Better to die than to let the Umayyads walk all over us…as Ali allows them to do. And he calls himself one of the rightfully guided caliphs," Muljam's eyes squinted almost closed against the sun's scorching rays. "You know the story."

"Not so many years ago, it happened. Ali was a young man then…and so you too. Once Angel Gabriel began to reveal the word of God to the Prophet, Muhammad moved his family and his congregation to a smaller city, Yathrib, just north of Mecca, where the town dwellers were interested in his one God religion. A large community of Jews and other tribes of various faiths lived in the

Yathrib and invited Muhammad to their town. They changed the name of their city to Medina."

Muljam's words reminded Salemad of the past. In those times, the Meccans did not care to convert to Muhammad's strange worship of Abraham's single god. Like the Jews and Christian Byzantines before him, the new Arab prophet had to form an army and wield a sword to persuade the many pagan tribes to the one and only God. It was then that Muhammad showed the many colors that painted his character. At moments he spoke and acted out of peace and charity, other times his temper raged and he swung a sharp scimitar. Like the Jews and the Christians, his new religion wore many faces for the One God.

Talking with Muljam, Salemad recalled how Muhammad had carried a fire in his belly. He'd insisted on one set of rules to match the one God. Though the Quraish and other tribes resisted, a few of the Bedouin tribes allied with Muhammad early on when they saw some benefits of a unified market for trading and a more powerful army under one God. When rumor spread over the dunes that Muhammad and his small Muslim militia were planning to raid the Quraish's caravan traffic, the Meccans launched and lost an attack on Medina, the battle of Badr, where Jews and other tribes fought bravely with the Muslims against the Quraish. The Muslims believed that their victory served as concrete proof of God's preference for them. He remembered how Muhammad had changed in many ways after his victories. He had become bold and decisive.

"Although he showed mercy to the men captured in battle of Badr," Muljam continued, "he grew confident, zealous. The Prophet said, 'We will move our direction of prayer, *qibla*, away from Jerusalem and now to Mecca, the new center of our faith.' He also promised his new army, saying, 'Any one of you soldiers of God, when you die fighting for your faith, I promise your soul ascends directly to heaven. Angels will welcome you battlefield martyrs. Young women, dark and large eyed virgins will surrender their pleasures to you and serve you bowls of the purest wine and fruits of your choice and flesh of the fowls you relish. These young women will please you eternally with their hidden pearls.' And now," Muljam shrugged and said, "that is why we, the Khawarijites, call Ali an unbeliever. He is not decisive. He fears the sword. But we Khawarijites know that *jihad* guides us on the path to eternal paradise…martyrdom…it is the obligation of every Muslim."

Salemad leaned forward in his saddle, remaining silent for a moment and then said, “At his base in Kufa, Ali is still the greatest caliph since Muhammad. He is wise enough not to lead Muslims in battle against Muslims.”

Salemad thought then about how, so many years ago, Muhammad knew how to sell this new path to eternal life by using the same name as the popular Mother Goddess—Alla. A merchant first and foremost, Muhammad realized that the pagans would accept the new One God by this name.

Instead of isolating his congregation from the persecution he encountered in Mecca, Muhammad joined the Yathribites, many of whom were Jews and pagans who later became Muslims and fought with other Muslims for the glory of God. But Salemad did not try to explain these things to Muljam.

“Is Ali strong…and wise?” Muljam’s face creased into a grimace. Then he fell silent a moment, looking into the horizon where the sun began to draw shadows over the dunes. “Why do you, a Sufi, stay here?” he asked. “Why remain a friend of Ali? You are going to leave soon?”

“When my spirit tells me to leave,” he replied.

"If you went far from here, it would do you good," said Muljam, nudging his mount. "A Sufi has no business here…you are not a Muslim. You are infidel." With that the man and mare galloped away.

Salemad followed the caravan trail along the *wadi*, the crusty river bed, and quickly reached the Euphrates which led him back to Kufa. The Khawarijite's words hung in his mind…a clear threat. Muljam's words set his nerves on edge. He thought of how this new conflict pitting Muslims against Muslims had greatly saddened Ali. But there was little Salemad could do about it. As a Sufi it should not be any concern of his. He only accepted the new and expanding Arab religion in order to blend in and to avoid conflict. That was the Sufi way…religion as a mere shell for appearances. Their only interest in this world was of the spirit.

The Khawarijites' battles were no concern of his. Least of all now that he had decided to return to Persia and to a more cosmopolitan, sophisticated city where there were fewer disputes over the trade routes and the rules God wanted to impose. Yet there was more to this Muljam. Many of his own people considered him vicious. Only if the Khawarijites became desperate would they follow an upstart like Muljam. Then it occurred to Salemad, with a man like Muljam, the Khawarijites could continue the unrest and incite more violence. *Ali's life is threatened*, he thought.

"I must inform Ali of this," he muttered.

#

The heat made Salemad meditative and reminded him of the day, some fifteen years earlier, when he tasted sweet tea with the Prophet.

"When I was a small boy," Muhammad had told him, "two angels came to me carrying a golden cup filled with snow. Snow in the desert…in summer." He smiled, sipped his tea and continued. "They had me lay flat on my back. Still awake, I watched them pull my heart out of my chest. I felt no pain. They washed away a black blood clot from my heart and placed it back in its place. They told me that the heart of all mortals contains a darkness. It's best to wash it away."

He enjoyed Muhammad's company then when the Prophet discussed mystical experiences. He shook his head now, thinking how much things had changed. He nudged his horse into a gallop, hurrying to warn Ali.

As he approached Kufa, the Sufi skirted the base of a hill range that lined the Euphrates. In the town, he slowed his horse to a trot, thinking of going directly to the mosque where he was sure to find Ali.

Around Kufa the water holes attracted all sorts of people. The locals lost patience with the caravan travelers, even though they were a source of income. Whatever water remained in summer, it attracted double numbers of animals drinking at the brooks and the wells around the growing city. Overcrowding at the water holes caused arguments. Despite the townsfolk's good nature, the hot season made them irritable. They did not hide their annoyance at the crowding. Smiles dropped from their faces. They lost all desire to socialize. Conflicts often flared up in the dry breeze, fights over the water, food, and ideas. Dogs dropped dead in the heat.

That summer the desert became a less endurable hell with each passing day. The sun grew oppressive, making the days pass slowly. Members of the Quraish tribe had come from as far away as Mecca in early spring, leading caravans and conducting trade. They had begun their trek back to Mecca but after only two days, they were forced back to Kufa where they sought grazing land for their animals.

Muhammad and his family had been Quraish for generations. The Quraish habitually followed the clouds, if there were any, and stopped wherever they found water to keep their animals alive. Well skilled in desert travel, they knew where to go at all times of the year, when to leave places and where to head next. The Quraish knew all the trade routes. Despite their skills in navigating the desert, they had to return to Kufa. The heat drove crowds of various tribes in from the wilderness to seek the town water.

The Sufi prodded his mount through the throngs of people and animals at the market. He took a dirt road that angled north where the great mosque of Kufa came into sight.

From a distance, he could see someone leaning in one of the main arched doorways. Another figure came from the dark shadows of the arcade that lined the outside of the rectangular main building, its outer wall served as a fortification to the inner mosque. Closer now, he found one of Ali's assistants, dismounted, and tied his horse to a post in the shade.

"*Allāhu Akbar*," he greeted the young man. "Have you seen Ali?"

"At the inner mosque," replied Ali's assistant, pointing into the courtyard through the archway.

He reached the inner mosque and approached a crowd of excited people shouting, and waving their hands in anger. He pushed through the pressing groups of men but could not reach the center of activity, the source of the commotion. Still squinting from the brightness outside, he forced his eyes wide to the interior dimness. He stood looking down the familiar corridor to the mosque but could not advance in the thick crowd. He edged his frame sideways, with effort, inching forward through the throng of men dressed in robes.

"What has happened?" he asked an elderly man.

"Someone attacked Ali Talib," the old man said, the deep wrinkles moving in small waves across his face like the drifting desert sands.

"Where is he now? Where is Ali?"

"They carried him off to see the physician." The old man waved his hand down a corridor. "They say someone cut him with a scimitar."

Salemad paced slowly backward several steps until his back brushed against a stone wall inside the corridors. He stood still shocked, his mind in a daze. Someone had attacked his friend Ali, the second most important leader of the new religion, Islam, the last of the four rightfully guided caliphs who had been personal assistants to Muhammad fighting for the new religion.

He stood stiff for a moment and then let his knees fold slowly beneath him. His back slid against the polished marble wall until he was sitting on the floor of the hallway. His heart strained in his chest. Tears rolled down his cheeks. Only hours ago he had spoken with Muljam on the caravan trail. Could he have run his mare directly here so fast to attack the caliph? His mind wandered through all the events of the day. He tore the turban from his head and let his long black hair fall over his face to hide his despair.

Slipping into a meditative stupor, he drifted through his memories. Suddenly he was in the marketplace where merchants came to sell and buy. When the Angel Gabriel began to whisper into

Muhammad's ear about the religion of the One God...of Abraham, Moses, and of Christ, he knew he'd have to sell it to his family and friends in that bazaar of rugs, foods, and ideas. Making that religion an Arabic one would unify all the tribes.

Merchants traveled in caravans, some from as far away as what was now called India. They frequently passed through Kufa and its fertile farmland, the Sawad, on their way to Mecca, a commerce hub of the Fertile Crescent, and stayed longer than at other times in Kufa, waiting for the moon to grow full, making it possible to travel at night rather than during the blistering day.

The Sufi slumped down on the floor, distraught, and recalled how, years earlier, Muhammad moved from Mecca to Medina, escaping the hostilities of pagan tribes. Islam remained in its infancy. Early on, most people considered Muhammad more a diplomat than a warrior. He avoided conflict. His relatives and neighbors, his own Quraish tribe, and residents of Mecca often cursed his name and yelled obscenities at him and his family. Children threw stones at him. Old women spat in his direction. Gangs of young men pushed and shoved him in the streets. Rather than retaliate, he would often recite the verses that Angel Gabriel had whispered in his ear.

"Unbelievers, I do not worship what you worship, nor do you worship what I worship. I shall never worship what you worship, nor will you ever worship what I worship. You have your own religion, and I mine."

Long after Muhammad began talking of the one God, most Arab tribes preferred to worship many gods, including the high Mother Goddess, Alla. She consorted with the Hindu God Siva…a shape shifter…sometimes taking the form of IL or other times ILLA, the name that sounded so much like Allah.

Salemad thought of the fantastic goddesses and gods in those times—their shifting forms would not allow mere mortals to settle in to any one way of thinking, no dogma, no fixed ideas. They inspired imagination and innovation, though when it came to unifying these nomadic tribes under a single belief, the gods—especially the nurturing, creative Mother Goddess—had little ambition. Muhammad loved everything about women and the goddesses that surrounded the region. Women lifted his spirits to moments of inspiration, but he was also a practical man. He wanted to organize and unify the Arab people under the one God.

As a Sufi many townsfolk called Salemad a mystic because he spoke intuitively of the human soul, not devoted to any one formal religion. Over time he befriended the leaders of the new Muslim movement. The Muslims often tried to claim parts of his Sufi mysticism into their belief, though most of them rejected the free spiritual thinking as esoteric innovations. He enjoyed hearing the many stories of Jesus' mystical teachings, though his thoughts on peace and love were often ignored. Now it occurred to him. Something similar had happened to Muhammad's teachings; many of his followers were interested only in organizing the religion as a source of power…empire. Muhammad had been an army general, prophet, mystic, political leader…all things at that time…a charismatic avatar.

In those days Muslims practiced Ramadan during the summer, celebrating the month when Muhammad received divine messages from Angel Gabriel which his cousin Ali had later written down as the Koran. The very name 'ramadan' derives from a term, 'to burn.' Fasting during this month was often thought of as a time to burn away all sins, to cleanse the soul and begin a new year. Muslims believed that the Koran was sent down to the earth during this month. Legend had it that Muhammad told his followers that the gates of Heaven would be open all month and the gates of Hell closed. Years later the month of fasting was moved to the cooler days of fall. Muslims used Ramadan as a time to strengthen ties with God.

Years later Muhammad returned to Mecca to battle the region's pagans, converting them by sword to God. Once he vanquished the pagans in Mecca and elsewhere, everyone said that God had blessed him as a chosen leader. His military victories were proof of his divine leadership as a holy man and impressed many of the nomadic tribesmen and greatly helped in their conversion. Once he had converted most of the Arabic peninsula, the new prophet died as if he had completed the purpose of his existence and found the proper moment to leave his body in this world and continue on to the next dimension, the one invisible to mortals.

That was when Salemad began to spend more time with Muhammad's cousin, Ali Talib. He remembered so clearly how one day, while sitting in the shade of the great mosque of Mecca, Ali told him, "Not a single verse of the Koran descended upon the Messenger of God, Muhammad, which he did not proceed to dictate to me and make me recite. I would write it with my own hand, and he would instruct me as to its *tafsir*—the literal meaning and the spiritual sense."

#

A full day passed before Ali had enough strength to ask for Salemad the Sufi. By then everyone knew that a Khawarijite had cut Ali with a poisoned blade. The Persian physicians arrived early in the morning from Baghdad and prescribed herbal antidotes, but none of them were optimistic. One of them, the eldest and most respected, suggested that Ali might have only another day to live and that there was no real antidote for the lethal poison in his blood.

"Salemad," said Ali, lying on a thick Persian bed cushion in his chamber, "you know I'm dying." Hardly had Salemad entered the room and Ali spoke to him with a low voice.

"I'm so sorry." He sat on a Persian rug next to Ali's soft cushion filled with feathers. "I came as fast as I could to warn you, to tell you that only an hour before the attack, I had talked with

Muljam out on the *wadi*, the one east of here at the edge of the Sawad."

"Do not fret over what God has allowed to happen," said Ali. "My time has come. I have arranged for my family to care for my wife, Fatima. Please, my last words for you, friend, I don't have much time. Fatima will return soon. I want this to be a secret between you and me because it is so important…all of Islam rides upon these simple verses. Anyone who knows about this secret runs many risks. Many people want to control this." Ali pulled a black box out from under his cushion. "You must leave now, take this. Keep it secret. Show it only to your most trusted and reliable friends in the Sufi Order."

"But Ali, I—"

"Please listen," Ali held a hand on his throat as if making a huge effort to speak. "I have little time left in this world. I trust you more than any man in my entourage, even after…especially since my friends have betrayed me. They pretend to live in the spirit of the Koran's equality, but they seek only power. They are radicals who turn their backs on the community. Please, take this, a piece from the Koran—a Sura—for which Muljam came to kill. They want to keep this out of the Koran. The Muawiyyah sect had sent him here. They want to control every aspect of what the Prophet Muhammad dictated to me. They see only the empire and want to reign over it. They do not care for the Kingdom beyond. Put the box under your robe and go quickly. Fatima will be here in a moment. I don't want her to know about this or even about you. Go far from here my friend. The Khawarijites may be only the beginning of those who use Islam only for its earthly powers. You will discover it is a Sura that the Umayyads have stripped from the Koran. It contains the verses of peace, love, and the sacredness of woman."

The Call to Duty

Four Years after September 11

Day after day, he went to work in a city where hundreds of bodies littered empty lots. Kris Klug kept a mental note of how the graffiti evolved on the walls of buildings in green or black paint—things like AVENUE OF DEATH, others scrawled in Arabic: INFIDELS GET OUT or NO OIL FOR AMERICA. In these neighborhoods, the mosques had become mini-fortresses with sandbagged rooftop fighting positions. Trash filled the streets, closed off by makeshift barriers of palm tree stumps, cinder blocks, and barbed wire. After more than a year in Afghanistan and more than a year of this work in the cesspool called Iraq, he began to wonder where it was all going.

Sergeant Kris Klug, Green Beret, team leader, that's who he was, and how he saw himself, at least until it ended. He often wrote home to his Uncle Fred, one of his only remaining family, about how Baghdad in August bred nasty thoughts and bad humor. Outside it was 120° Fahrenheit. Inside a Stryker armored truck, temperatures rose to 130°, sometimes 140°. The regular grunts that manned the Strykers sweated as though they cooked in a kettle. Their pants showed damp marks wherever they brushed against their skin. The sweat dripped off their eyebrows and collected in their goggles.

Hot desert winds would often waft up thick dark gray clouds of sand and blast everything. During the sandstorms war would stop but the heat intensified—it balled up in a fist and no one could go about their business of killing and looting.

The civil war had already begun, just that nobody wanted to admit it, nobody in politics wanted to say it. The first neighborhood they secured was Ghazaliya, a Sunni area in western Baghdad. Kris's team was the first to enter the area and feed information back for the Stryker teams. Sunnis had always been hostile to the U.S. presence. Though, some of the people seemed suspiciously happy to see Americans. It was the first time in weeks they'd been able to open up their stores and walk outside. But they always kept an eerie distance. A gulf separated them even when they exchanged a cigarette or some other social gesture. The gap between the occupiers and the occupied dried into a crusty, palpable layer of distrust and resentment. Some Iraqis would come outside, looking pale and blinking in the bright sunlight. On every block houses stood empty, and the stench and sludge of sewage spewed through the streets where the upper crust of Iraqi society once prospered.

Kris's unit moved in the shadows and passed enough information to the Stryker teams, the grunts, so they could move in and hit the right priorities. In three mosques the soldiers had uncovered weapons used to attack Americans and Shiites. In the Al-Sadiq mosque, used by the Iraqi Islamic Party, they found IED's buried in the courtyard and mortars hidden in the minarets. The beauty of the ornate mosaics in the mosques could deceive one into calm, spiritual thoughts. At another Sunni mosque they discovered a beheading knife. They rummaged through the Iraqi Islamic Party's headquarters and turned up bombs covered by sandbags or first-aid kits. They found coffins used to smuggle weapons and documents detailing how the IIP was running death squads.

For the Army grunts, today was different. They received orders to work directly with a special-forces unit. Kris knew this would help boost the morale all around, that's why he pushed his commanders for it.

At 0500, he met with the squad leaders. "We're going in to take a suspect, a former major general of the Fedayeen Army. We've gathered intelligence proving that he's dealing and organizing attacks on coalition forces. The mission's code name is Ruby."

"What's the code for after we've got Ruby?" One of the squad leaders took off his helmet and rubbed the top of his scalp.

"Cucamonga," Kris responded and watched the Strykers drive out of the forward base to their rendezvous spot near the point of operation.

The Army gunner squad waited in their Strykers on the side of the road near empty lots. Birds worked over the bodies of dead Iraqis that lay there in the early morning, victims of historical blunders. The sight and stench of rot made one soldier puke so loud it scared one of the vultures off from a good meal.

Kris's team drove in a beat up minivan, looking like a group of average Iraqis on their way to work. The guys in the Strykers dropped the back ramp to talk. In awe of the Special Forces guys, the grunts eagerly offered cigarettes and conversation—but no time for that.

Although Kris hid his emotions well, his stomach leaped into his throat as he exited the dirty vehicle and walked up to talk with the platoon sergeant. "It's a go." He scratched his bearded chin and gave the signal to his team to deploy. They disappeared silently on foot up an alley behind a group of crumbling houses built from gray, unpainted cinder blocks. Adrenaline rushed through his veins and he seemed to walk a little above the ground.

The Stryker teams took position. Their role was to stand guard and provide backup in case anything went sour. They parked the Strykers in a muddy field covered with garbage and dismounted from the armored vehicles. The neighborhood dogs immediately started barking at them.

Ropes and wooden braces propped up many of the cinder block houses. The entire neighborhood had fallen into decay. It bordered on the notorious Ghazaliya area. Kris's team was already behind "Ruby's" house.

Maybe it was the noise of the dogs. Maybe it was the presence of the Army squads walking down the street. By the time the Stryker squad approached the front of Ruby's house, the man had already scrambled out the front door and had grabbed a woman who was walking with a little girl. He held a gun to the woman's head. She cried and clung tightly to her little girl. Ruby used them as shields from the Stryker squad.

Looking all the way through the house's windows from the back alley out to the street, Kris could see that the squad took positions along the curb, right in front of the house, close to a street corner. There was nothing they could do. If they approached Ruby or tried to take a shot at him, they jeopardized the panic-stricken woman and her girl.

Kris and his team had already scrambled into the house silently through the back door. He could see Ruby walking slowly up the street away from the house while holding the hostages in front of him. One of Ruby's bodyguards bolted out of the house, fleeing Kris's team. The man pulled a Makarov 9mm pistol and took a shot at one of the soldiers, who fell to the ground, blood spilling from his face. Aw shit. Enough of this crap. He felt his gut tie into a knot when he saw his guys getting hit. He moved on reflex.

Kris moved fast to the front door, looking for a clear angle. The commotion woke up some of the neighbors; flickering gaslights went on in some of the houses, even though the sun had begun to rise. He stood frozen in the doorframe, adrenaline coursing through him. He raised his M16 to his shoulder. First he put a bullet square in the middle of the bodyguard's back before the man could squeeze off another round.

Then he turned to Ruby. The only clear shot he had at him was the man's left shoulder, farthest away from the woman and child. He had to take a shot now that he'd drawn attention. In the blink of an eye, he bent his knees, steadied himself against the doorframe and seized the moment. He pulled the trigger, spun Ruby around, and laid him out on the cobblestone street. Kris jumped on him, folded his knee on the back of his neck and flattened him to the ground. The woman ran away with the little girl in her arms. Gun smoke scented the morning air.

Small explosions went off inside the house. Kris pinned Ruby face down and tightened plastic restrainers around his wrists.

He heard thrashing and yelling from inside the house. His team was clearing the building of Ruby's own guards. Then the minivan drove up to where Kris stood. Another one of Ruby's guards stormed out of the front door, firing an automatic pistol at Kris and the gunner teams.

The Stryker teams returned fire and the guard fell within seconds.

A bullet struck the ground near Kris, ricocheted through his left shoulder and clipped off part of his ear. Larry Larson, another one of the Green Berets in Kris's team, grabbed Ruby and freed Kris to get help for his wound.

A medic pulled him into one of the Strykers, where he could give him some first aid. He was not seriously injured but needed to go to the hospital to check against infection and patch up what was left of his ear.

Kris wasn't even winded, although his insides chilled as the adrenaline flames turned into some nervous ice and the cold sweat was always there and unwelcome after a mission. He stepped mechanically through the mission sequence and called out the

"Cucamonga" message over the Icom radios. He switched to the minivan he'd come in. It was all over in less than fifteen minutes.

Everyone loaded up and rolled out with the dead bodyguards, who had tried to defend their leader.

Larson seated Ruby next to Kris. Ruby had a weight problem and wore a gray man-dress. Now, the captive sported a blue sandbag over his head.

"Scoot your fat butt over!" Larson jabbed Ruby in the ribs with his fist. "We're going to give you some payback for September 11."

Kris thought to say how the guy was probably just as surprised about September 11. Iraqis had nothing to do with terrorists, at least until we'd invaded the country. But he didn't say anything. He just held pressure to the gauze that the medic had taped to his ear. Damn that hurt. Just another day in this hellhole Iraq.

The Dog **Don't** Hunt

Jean was the eldest of a family of four girls and the fifth, a long awaited boy. Though, she was different. Her father had been handsome and no good and Jean had learned this from the moment she could comprehend sentences. People said that John Wallace, with his hazel-green eyes and wavy sandy hair, shinning with strains of Scottish red, had captured the notice of all the single women in Klamath County and, once he arrived on the scene, he had become the man about the dance halls, knocked up at least one single woman after a dance, a situation that hastened a civil wedding.

The man left a month after Jean was born, heading back home to Canada where he occasionally mentioned that he had obligations with the military service. When he kissed his young wife and baby daughter good night as he did every evening, he told them he loved them. Cutting out the next morning at the break of dawn, he had become a mystery, the father she'd never known except through the stories she had heard her whole life, growing up on a small farm. She had heard it all, heard it many times and in the telling of it, people embellished form one version to the next until the truth could not be separated from the legend. More than this, the legend had set her apart, making the past a shackle on her ankle in the present.

Her father had disappeared in the north, and Jean's mother, Evelyn, always told some version of the story how the man had to serve his country or face prison, how she watched the shadow of a man slinking out one frosty spring morning, hopping into his rusted 1920 Ford model T Touring car whose fenders and windshield were broken off and never returned.

It was the same day the only radio station in Klamath Falls had played *Hallelujah Bum Again* over and over, and Evelyn had listened to the radio news flash about a group of Italians who failed in their attempt to assassinate a dictator by the name of Mussolini. It was a Sunday, Jean remembered because her mother always talked about that day when she was so sad she swaddled her baby Jean up in wool blankets and rode with the neighbors to the nearby Baptist Church in Keno and learned that the Baptist Church had founded the

Clear Creek Baptist Bible College as an institution of higher education somewhere in Kentucky. Evelyn remembered that detail whenever she told the story, not because she had any inkling about higher education, but because her father had grown up in Kentucky and moved out to Oregon long ago and had taken a job to drive a stage coach back and forth between Klamath Falls and Redding.

At the Southern Baptist Church, Evelyn cradled her baby girl in her bosom, listening at first to the choir singing hymns and then to Pastor Davy preaching about craving, burning, passions that drag the soul into the red, smoldering ambers of hell. Evelyn shuddered at the pastor's authoritarian and detailed depictions of carnal sin. She knew no more overwhelming anxiety than to be judged as the mother of a bastard daughter.

That day, the few friends she had made at the church talked after the pastor's sermon about how the radio had a corrupting influence on the human soul, how country western, and especially the dark, moody music of black jazz musicians should be banned from the public ear. As time passed without any sign of Jean's father, Evelyn's church friends spoke at growing frequency of the increasing numbers of illegitimate children in Klamath County.

"They hear about free love in the new fangled radio songs and before you know it, everyone thinks it's normal," said Pastor Davy during his sermon.

She thought of selling her Victor 17 radio, which someone had given her after its oak case had been damaged in a house fire.

"It's my only source of entertainment," Jean said to one of her sisters, "at night after the chores are done. I'm alone out here. I might as well get some use out of that electric line now that it comes all the way out here." She explained how it was her only source of information from the world outside the backwater farm country of the Klamath Basin. "Since I got electrical current in the house, might as well go ahead and keep the radio at least for the occasional cultural programs. That *Amos and Andy* comedy show is pretty good."

"I'll stay and watch Jean," Evelyn's sister, Rita, who schemed a little plan to help find a new husband for her. "You go into town with the others. They're going to the dance hall every Saturday night. You go and find yourself a good, solid husband. Get this whole thing put in the past, water under the bridge. People can stop talkin' about this situation. That John Walker's been away for more than three years now. He won't be back."

Only a few months after Jean's second birthday, Evelyn had inherited an acre or so after the death of her father. All six of the children received a piece of the farm. "It's the thing," said Rita to Evelyn, "that will make the deal more attractive. You go to town and find a hard working man—the one can hold up his end of the table, provide for a family."

In a day when the mourning time was a month for a lost wife and two years for a husband gone disappearing, Evelyn decided it was proper to follow her sister's sage advice. She came from a line of Yurok Indians in southern Oregon and from a line of French trappers who grew restless and wondered to the west coast after most of their community had settled in Kentucky. Shiny dark hair was in her genes, she made an early mother at seventeen. Farm-raised and conditioned for pragmatic life, she counted her new daughter as a blessing from divine light and took the hard thankless work of raising a baby alone as a test. She loved the baby's warm little hands and soft skin. From childhood she'd known mostly hard farm work without praise and the Southern Baptist Church gave her a source of spiritual support in tough moments, her only source of culture and education. Farming had taught her the benefits of being strong and resourceful. It didn't take her long to find another husband, a reliable, hard-working one.

Jean's new father, Edward, accepted her and she put in the extra effort to be accepted through endless labor. She learned to force good humor until she no longer recognized it from real happiness.

Evelyn loved Edward the more she learned how special he was, able to accept a infant daughter, another mouth to feed, without regret. He had his own handicap which only taught him to be more tolerant of others. He stood tall and handsome with thick sandy hair and a big smile. He had dabbled in bull-riding as a teenager and a bad fall had broken his knee. Having been a wild one in his youth, he often regretted stupid things he had done. Regrets often pulled him down into dark moods that prompted him to drink. Only a month before he and Evelyn married, he landed a good paying job at Weyerhaeuser Lumber Company. Prosperity blessed the new family. Three more baby girls had come until finally, old Edward planted just the right seed and sired a son whom he named Edward. Years passed and old Edward's knee stiffened with arthritis in the cold climate but he cowboyed up and didn't bitch about it, and kept his job even after he'd lost his left thumb to a buzz-saw. It was the volume of beer he consumed that helped him to tolerate the pain of farming life, the nagging weight of people's gossip about Jean for whom he never showed the slightest affection.

At times when the alcohol got to him, he cursed his adopted daughter as the fruit of evil. She took it in stride as her cross to bear and listened to the aging Pastor Davy who gave sermons about the sins of passionate flesh. Most everyone took it on faith that the good Pastor was the Christ come back from the dead and they lived close to the sacred words of their true prophet.

By the 1940's, everyone had crawled out of the Great Depression and men were finally coming home from the war. Spring of 1948 was one of the hardest times. Hungry coyotes had been slipping into the barn, stealing the chickens. One morning old Ed tracked down a couple of the four-legged thieves and moved in close enough to take a shot at them with his 12 gauge, but just as he aimed, one of his feet broke through a deep snow drift. The gun blasted next to his ear and took away almost all his hearing.

Evelyn knew it was high-time that Jean found a husband. Old Ed was aging, growing almost feeble, and his loss of hearing being the first stumble into a slowing life where he was hardly able to support all five kids.

Old Ed was a white trash farmer and a boozer, said Claude Wester, eyes squinting behind thick plastic rimmed glasses, and not so much that his farm was small, but because an old horse pulled plow sat rusting next to the creek and the barn's paint had chipped off down to the naked, warping pinewood, and because old Ed had married into the farm without earning it by his own merits of hard work and industry, instead he just accepted a bastard daughter. That dog don't hunt, said Claude often to his buddies down in the town coffee shop, talking about old Ed behind his back.

Old Ed ignored the neighbors' talk and spent most of his time in the garden during the sunny days and drank beer any other time. Everyone around had heard Claude's jokes about how the old dog don't hunt and now the dog don't hear.

Jean obediently followed her mother's advice. After frequenting the dance hall in Keno, she found an eligible man who seemed solid and hard-working, even one with farming experience from Nebraska since before the Dust Bowl.

Karl had learned new trade skills as a mechanic in the CC camps which he developed further during the long years in European theater. The young couple had settled in Klamath Falls and enjoyed months of romantic picnic trips in the Green Springs until Jean's first pregnancy and the first frosts of fall. The first born was a son and Karl began to spend more hours at his job with the gas station on Highway 66, the old Green Springs road.

He always operated some business on the side of a regular job. The first couple of years he hauled lumber at night down the mountain to Klamath Falls. By then they already had two boys and a baby girl, Kay, a green-eyed blondie who took little time to walk and grow tall as a bean stock. Jean favored her. Karl had little time for staying at home. He had five mouths to feed and tried to make ends meet, succeeding in starting his own automobile repair shop, specializing in automatic transmissions on the bleeding-edge of automotive technology.

He was proud to get out of farming, moving up to a better paying technical job. Still he had to burn the night oil, hauling lumber after a day at his business. To avoid paying taxes, he decided to deliver the lumber without receipts, no paper trail meant no taxes.

"Had me a bad turn of luck," he told Jean one day. "A whole month of wages hauling lumber. The lumber yard won't pay me because I didn't take the damn receipts," he said as he pulled out a wax paper pouch of tobacco and rolled his own cigarette, with a mournful face, a cloud of smoke rising up around his head. "Got my head caught in yoke with that deal."

"One thing after another," she said wearily. She pulled at a thread protruding from a seam in a shirt she had just pieced together by recycling the course gunny sack tissue that had contained potatoes, one shirt for each of the two little boys.

"You know what the foreman said?" he asked.

She looked at him wondering where his latest story was headed.

"He said my dog don't hunt."

When she heard the expression, her face blanched and she turned for the kitchen. Both of them shared the special understanding behind the phrase.

She went to the sink, stepping over Hound, Karl's old Labrador he had brought home a few days after the second boy arrived into their world. She began peeling the ten potatoes for diner.

"It's just an expression," he said while tapping his cigarette into the ashtray on the bare linoleum kitchen table.

"Not much luck lately, moneywise," she said, setting a pot of water over a gas flame on the stove.

"A guy's gotta have a knack for certain things," he said and shrugged.

She never could figure him out, even after the first nine years. With Karl Luster everything a man did depended on knack and he was still finding his. His secret boyhood ambition had been to become a poet, a cowboy poet, even a charismatic radio personality. He had memorized all sorts of poems by famous poets like Robert Service. His father was a strong, tough German whose family line tracked all the way to Iceland. Long ago, back in Nebraska his father had bought a radio in a large oak case about the size of a vegetable crate. It had huge tubes like baby bottles but they glowed when anyone looked through the air vent slots in the back. From a high-watt station in Lincoln, he could tune into the cowboy shows. He especially loved Fred and Mel Allen, Jack Benny, and later, above all, Roy Rogers who was only seven years older than he.

Though work on the home farm kept his dream at a faded distance stretching out over the vast ocean of corn and wheat. For fun he made toys for his younger sisters and brothers. Otherwise, his chores came first and school work second. His father was a joyless, hard-working man, who never spent a minute for fun, least of all with his kids whom he trained for constant labor.

Jean was attracted to him because they shared similar backgrounds. She could relate and she resented that, not five miles down the road from the first house they'd bought, Claude Wester's son, Chuck had enjoyed every advantage, inheriting the large farm from his father. From boyhood Chuck had gone to the finer private schools and traveled abroad and stayed out of the war, claiming that he had other priorities in keeping the family business going, supplying the troops with food.

As Janice and the two boys grew up, Karl's auto-repair business staggered along and, when TransCo Corporation established cheap transmission repair service chain across the country, the wheels fell off his small shop. Jean fretted and did her best to make ends meet until she and Karl decided to move to warm California where jobs were plenty.

He found few moments of free time when she could smoke a Camel cigarette and meditate on the day.

Once they settled into then new stucco tract house, in a burgeoning urban town of Stockton. Karl would leave at the break of dawn and return at dinner time to listen to the news on television, look over the newspaper and do a crossword puzzle. The change to warm climate eased the pain of arthritis in his knee damaged in the war.

Jean prepared the meals like clock-work. Years passed easily in the smooth wear of routine. The kids went to school. Jean did the housework and enjoyed her new life far from the family and the harsh memories of her origins in the backwater farm. The less she thought of the abuse as a bastard, the less it hurt her now. the calm routine of life helped her to forget.

But then the kids began to reach that age. It irritated Jean that Kay had little interest in the Girl Scouts.

"They're all rich kids," she said. "I don't fit in their clicks."

It was in the air, Jean recognized how her own sensitivities wore off onto her own daughter like a curse from the old two cow, three chicken farm she'd left in Oregon. Jean could always come up with chores for her young daughter whether emptying the trash or cleaning her room, or taking the little dog out for a walk.

Washing the dishes was the worst for Kay. She would hardly clean off the pieces of potatoes stuck to the plates and she would let them dry without wiping them.

Occasionally inspired by some vague inclination for affection, Kay might try to hug Jean who would be working on his ceaseless quest for a sparkling clean house. Jean would ignore the closeness like a strange, even perverted impulse somehow even frightening sexual, a distraction from the endless chores.

Once in a while Kay wondered off, walking around the neighborhood, going all the way to the park near the strip-mall where young men gathered to drink wine or beer at the cement picnic benches.

Herself, Jean never went for a walk, never had time for it, considered it inappropriate for a married woman, mother of a family, a wasteful distraction from her duty, a sort of unspoken disloyalty to her husband who was still at work. She devoted her energies to washing the clothes and linen in the electric washing machine and dryer, vacuuming the carpet, mopping the linoleum on the kitchen floor. The two boys and Karl always tracked dirt into the house and her endless, thankless job was to keep things tidy.

Karl was most often relaxing in his recliner chair taking a nap if he wasn't at work at the truck company, repairing Peterbuilts or doing odd jobs under the table by fixing cars for peole at hime in the garage. The war had left him with shrapnel in his flesh and a bad case of narcolepsy.

"Had me a bad day today," he said, slipping into his old recliner just under the air-conditioner after a long day, repairing trucks in the heat of the San Joaquin Valley.

She waited, always interested in his stories of work outside the house. She was often hesitant to venture out then, wary of what people might think of her and still not accustomed to driving a car even after many years, and despite her secret wish for independence.

"Foreman chewed me out," he said, "had a trucker mad at me. The clutch I replaced wasn't adjusted quite right. He had to turn his rig around and bring it back into the shop for another hour.

She nodded, listening carefully, but there was little more she could do. “Well, you can’t get it right all the time.” She said in her consoling voice. They had always been somehow connected

She nodded, listening carefully, but there was little more she could do. “Well, you can’t get it right all the time.” She said in her consoling voice. They had always been somehow connected at some level, if only by the affinities of similar pasts and origins and the passage of years and growth of their own off-spring.

Not a man of many words, he seldom ever expressed his emotions, except as a subtext in his stories.

She scraped potato skins and sliced the naked white vegetables thin for frying. She was always dressed properly with her shoes on even though she seldom stepped out of the house. She kept her shoes on because she was horrified to open the door to visitors in her bare feet, echoing back to shameful memories of tending to the cows in the marsh lands, barefoot.

“And then, coming back from work,” he said, “I got a flat tire ‘n had to stop to change out the spare.”

“Well,” she said, “you’re good for the rest of the week. Got all the bad stuff done and put away.”

She worried about him, but never showed it much. She worried about how his narcolepsy was worsening, how he had to sleep more and more, how it affected his work. Only last week, she took Kay to the department store to buy her school supplies and, by chance, he was out in the parking lot repairing a big sixteen-wheeler, the heat baring down, melting the asphalt, sweat running down his face, and him running back and forth to get tools from his utility van. No wonder he had suffered a mild heart attack two years ago and laid up in the hospital for four days. Their health insurance did not cover so much and they had to pay the difference. The war had left him in bad health, but he never talked about the terror of his combat experience and kept whatever photos he took of those times and the souvenirs in a hidden trunk in the attic.

Then, too, she often remembered fondly about the carefree days they spent together enjoying the sunshine and pleasures of a picnic in the Green Spring hills. Those were joyous times, worth a lifetime of memories.

She wondered now how she would go on if anything ever happened to him.

###

By the time Kay started High School, her two older brothers had already finished and moved on to Junior College in town, still living at home. She was sure they didn't like being around her. They never did anything with her, no movies, no trips out for fun at the hamburger shop, no trips to the skating rink downtown.

Home was a new house located at the northern edge of the city, built on a wood frame, concrete foundation, and stucco facing at the end of a street bordering open fields of farm land full of rice, wheat, sugar-beats, and tomatoes.

When she started High School, she learned what she'd already learned from her older brothers, that few people would be her friend, that she was hardly worthy of friends and only the dejected chose her, she had little choice.

Jean helped her pick out nice clothes for her first year. "You'll have to make these last the year," she said to Kay. "Prices are going up and your Dad's wages stay the same."

She had few choices in clothes so they picked out blue jeans, blouses and a nice cotton dress.

She learned that the rules of social etiquette bumped up a notch at high school. Everyone judged everyone. Kids were becoming adults, practicing the social habits of their parents, and she quickly learned that the sensibilities of a small farm girl that she inherited from her mother did not mix well with the sophisticated California city kids. Most of them had already become experts in sex, drugs, and rock'n roll.

"They're all nuts at the school," said Kay after the first three months. "They all act like they're Hollywood actors, driving fancy foreign cars and wearing sunglasses, and make-up."

"Well, they can't all be the same," said Jean, worried how her daughter might get caught up in the bad influences. "You'll find friends you like, just be patient."

"They're all four-point-oh, rich kids," I don't like it."

"Just concentrate on your school work," said her mother, "You'll find friends. What's a four-point-oh?"

"The creeps who get straight A's in all their classes," said Kay, "I don't like them."

Tall and thin with long straight blond hair, and green eyes, Kay filled out and caught the attention of boys. She decided to start wearing make-up like most of the other girls. Only a couple years earlier, Kay's parents had paid a fortune to have her teeth straightened. They had removed her only obstacle to find a perfect husband and move on with life.

Kay knew her father had worked extra hours to pay for her perfect teeth. His insurance didn't pay for orthodontics. He had to take afterhours and weekend jobs repairing cars in the garage attached to the house. The neighbors frowned on the home style entrepreneurialism, but he had to make ends meet. Kay heard the unspoken expectation that she should find a good husband to provide for her.

"You're always breathing down my neck," said Kay in her whining little voice. "How can I make any friends like this?"

She always resented that her mother watched over her as if she had no judgment of her own. Her mother kept the doors and windows closed to her social life since forever. "What are you afraid of?" she always asked. "You think I'll end up like your mother, right?" For this she never got an answer from her mother and this wore her down, dragging her to the limits of her teenage patience.

Kay complained to one of her first made friends at high school, a girl, Susan Hart, who fixed her hair in a frizzy style and wore gaudy jewelry and mismatched gypsy clothes like the blues singer, Janice Joplin.

"She doesn't let me go out to parties. No dating, no concerts, nothing."

"What's her problem?" asked Susan.

"She wants to keep me locked up," said Kay. "Just as well, though, the guys around here are dorks."

At the beginning of her second year, she did manage to find a nice young man. She brought him home one day and he wanted to meet her parents. He made a great impression on them.

"He's the nicest young man," her mother said. "You could go to the prom with him in you senior year. We could find a nice long, white dress for you to wear. Go dancing."

Kay, knowing she didn't have much to offer anyone, unworthy of good friends, was eager to follow the lead of whatever companions she could find.

The romance was cut short, though, when Kay's eldest brother, in a fit of jealousy, got into a shouting match with the poor boy who left quickly with a reddish face of mortified fear and embarrassment.

By the end of her second year, she had hit bottom. Confused and angry, her only consolation was the new and exciting experience she found in smoking weed that her pal, Susan, managed to purchase by some unknown and mysterious means. At first the pot smoking clamed her nerves and helped her to cope. But then, she barely passed her classes.

The summer before her senior year, she found herself hungry beyond what any drug could remedy. Ready to love anyone who would take her, a skinny boy with long black hair and always dressed in boots and a leather jacket, no matter what the weather, Sam Fick, noticed her, attracted to her sarcastic talk and her naïve Bambie eyes. At first, she answered to his occasional greetings with long, shy stares. When she thought he wasn't paying attention to her in history class, she daydreamed of long tight hugs and sweeping kisses.

One day in art class, the teacher, Mr. Labowski, assigned his students to write an essay on any modern artist. Daydreaming of Sam while flipping pages in the school library, Kay found the image of Salvador Dali, and read about his devoted love for his wife. She thought she saw Sam Fick looking up from the page, the intense eyes, the mocking, high-brow expression, the little mustache, standing straight in a dignified way. Now in her daydream, they traveled to Paris, visiting art galleries and holding hands in cafes that lined the Seine River. He took her far away from the agonizing, confined life.

Sam quickly acquired that haughty demeanor and let his hair and mustache grow longer and began to draw surrealistic images of Kay in desert landscapes with clocks melting over cactuses which reached their branches up like arms to a deep blue sky where angels soared and swopped in the dry, scorching air.

Aside from the surrealism, Kay and Sam began to act like a couple although Kay didn't really feel she should have a boyfriend, like they were a married couple, meeting at their book lockers in the hallway, setting next to each other in whatever classes they could take together. She was sure he was the one. And he was the only one. Her life long love, her only means to escape and move on with her life. She loved him and carried a photo of him in her purse, but kept him a secret at home.

At the end of their senior year, Sam asked Kay to a party. He had already found a part-time job at an art supply store and had moved into a three bedroom apartment with two other roommates, buddies from school. He had ambitions to become a photographer and artist. “Not to the prom,” he said. “To a party at my place. Maybe you could move in, live with us.”

She didn’t bother to talk about it with Jean. She expected her parents would fume in anger. So she just said that she was going to the prom with a friend and there was no need to buy any special dress.

No judge of character, Kay had made up her mind that Sam was her man come rain or high water. She gauged him as a solid and reliable man.

Before the last day of school, he said, “Let’s get married this summer.”

She smiled and kissed him on the lips and caressed his groin like never before. She could fee his member stiffen. It first happened in his car, late afternoon. She never imaged it would feel like that. It was uncomfortable in the back seat of his Gran Torino. She wanted more, and it would probably be more enjoyable doing it inside. She thought of his apartment, his bed.

The afternoon before the prom, she still let her parents believe that she was going to it and not to Sam's little party.

"You have someone to dance with?" asked Karl. He had usually avoided talking much with Kay. Growing up on a farm with a distant, cold father, he often seemed awkward when dealing with his own kids, unsure how to relate since he himself had hardly an example to follow from his own childhood.

"Yeah," she said. "I've got a friend, Sam. We'll dance and hang out. I'll be back late."

"Good for you, darling, I hope you have a wonderful time," he said in jovial tones, unlike his usual temperament. She understood him well enough that he loved his daughter, but his own childhood, and his combat experiences had sucked most joy out of him.

His encouragement and approval was maybe the closest to any praise he had ever given her, or so it seemed to her at the time. And she was confused just then. Her mother remained calm and quietly smoked a cigarette. She sensed that her mother, Jean, was skeptical of the whole course of events. Even then she let a wave of disappointment flow over her self-awareness, wondering why she had not done better in school, why she had not become friends with Chuck. He was going to the prom with someone else now.

She knew that Chuck was going to college next year, studying finance. He wanted to become a banker.

She pulled on her leather boots and headed out the door. No sense in thinking about spilled milk, she had to move on in life, to be free, independent, not some wife closed off in housekeeping. There must be some nuance between the two extremes, maybe it was already too late to sort it all out. Everything was changing so fast. Her Dad was not doing so well, getting tired. He needed to retire. She needed to get out of the house.

In a red Volkswagen bug her Dad had bought for her a year ago, she drove off to Sam's house, listening, to her favorite singer, Janice Joplin, "freedom's just another word for nothin' left to lose." She wondered that maybe her parents were relieved that she was finally finding her way in life, becoming an adult. Uneasiness flashed through her, and she said to herself while the music played, they don't know how I feel, don't know what it's like to be me.

All she knew was that she and Sam were engaged. Some kind of celebration was in order. Same agreed to meet her at the Kentucky Fried Chicken restaurant where she had been working part time for the last six months. Sam was already there with his two buddies, Derik and Kris, sipping beer. He had brought a six pack in from his car and sat there picking a sore at the side of his mouth when Kay arrived, excited about her little engagement party. She wore her nicest dress that hugged her slim body. A little silver chain belt around her thin waist accentuated her womanly hips. Her long beautiful legs set off by black high heels. She had brushed her long blond hair straight and tied it with a single green ribbon to match her dress and her eyes.

They told Mr. Dosh, the manager of the KFC diner, that they were celebrating their engagement and he gave them ten percent off their chicken. Sam and his two pals washed their chicken breasts down with a second beer from the six-pack he casually hid beneath a newspaper next to him on the bench in their booth. Kay drank a root-beer and ate a couple of thighs. Sam rose to leave and his friends followed with grins, leaving their empty beer bottles, paper plates and balled up greasy napkins on the table. Out of respect for Mr.

Dosh, Kay cleared the table and put the waste in the trash. Mr. Dosh smiled and waved as she approached to pay and said he would just deduct the bill from her pay check.

Back at his apartment, Sam put music on loud. Kay danced with him, then Kris danced with her and so, too, Derik. Sam pulled out a few little red pills, "Reds," he said and offered four to Kay. "They're good, make you relax and enjoy. Wash them down with a bottle of Heineken." He danced on with Kay whose legs weakened and her head spun a little in a dizzy whirl, everything seemed to move in slow motion. She took off her shoes. Derik helped her take off her belt.

Kris helped her take off her panty hose. That's when all three boys got naked. Everything seemed to blur but she felt so calm and relaxed even though what the boys were doing didn't seem right, she let herself go. She always wanted love, craved affection, now she was the center of attention. It was like basking in the sun after years of cold, cloudy winters. Somehow it might not be right, but the Quaaludes softened her will, euphoria spread over her body and for once she discovered a long ignored sensuality. First up was Sam, then Derik took his turn, and by the time Kris enjoyed her, she considered them all one with her, a family of love. Though, her thoughts were murky and dreamy, like stepping into a Dali scene.

When she woke up the next morning, it was Sam who rolled her over and caressed her from behind. She sensed pleasure, confusion, and a new, vague arousal. Somewhat disoriented, she heard Derik behind her and on top of her. Sam kissing her on the mouth and Kris caressing her, she soaked it all up without resistance allowing her normal world melt around her.

Out of a mixture of many emotions, mostly a growing shame, some pleasure, and disappointment, she stayed in the apartment for five days. The boys came and went but mostly stayed, watched TV, ate sandwiches with her and continued their little love fest.

When she came to her senses, not sure what to do next, she drove her Bug back to her home in the middle of the day and sat under the shower for more than an hour.

Months went by, Kay kept working at Mr. Dosh's KFC diner and he put her on full-time. She often worked over-time. The routine and fatigue of work kept her mind busy. She didn't want to think. She started wearing loose jeans and sports sweaters and gained weight, ignoring her body, her memories, and her feelings.

Almost a year passed, she had not seen Sam or his pals again. Her parents announced that they were selling the house to retire in Oregon, she followed them in her Bug.

Once moved in to the mobile home retirement community, she tried going to a vocational school to become a secretary. She received high grades all the way through the program, but a couple weeks before her certification, she decided she didn't fit with that sort of job. She took to drinking cheap wine and eating potato chips.

Years passed and life seemed to move on like the cars and trucks on Highway 5, not far from the retirement community. She didn't know why but she didn't feel like doing much of anything at all. She became buddies with her father who taught her how to make toys and wind chimes from wood.

Instead of rock'n roll, she started tuning into country western radio stations. She listened to songs about lonely people, dying from a broken heart. She heard a doctor once talk about how gaining fat can cause cancer.

Not a year passed and she began to feel faint all the time. Her father always drove her to regular chemotherapy sessions. He would take her in his old pickup truck and stop in the parking lot waiting for her to drive her back home. After each of the chimo sessions, she became increasingly feeble, barely able to walk back to her father waiting in his pickup.

At the funeral, Jean cried until not a tear was left inside her. It was then that Karl remembered watching Kay walk across that parking lot, every step as painful as death. He watched her thinking of the phrase, “The dog don’t hunt.” He went home and, though it took two long years, he cried himself to death.

Highway Cowboy

Solumund Sigurborn is born in Redding, California, May 4, 1951, the first of five. In 1954 his parents move to Klamath Falls where his mother's family lives. They settle into a Sears Roebuck's two-story house with six apple trees in the back yard. His father, Jens, is still struggling with the nightmares left from WWII combat. Little Solumund learns to sing "Pop Goes the Weasel." His father smacks him up-side the head with a rolled newspaper to shut him up. Mostly a gentle man, Jens falls into irascible moods at times. War gave him an edge that takes years to shake. He comes from a line of frost-bitten Icelandic stock, the same kind that pillaged and plundered most of northern Europe and traded with the Indians when hardly anyone else in Europe had dreamed the world was round and with a continent a Portuguese discoverer would later call America.

The high cheeks in Solumund's face and the dark shade of his otherwise blond hair are the only traits from his mother who was part Scottish, part Yurok Indian. His thick neck, round face, blue eyes, and tall husky body recall the seafaring plunderers in his father's lineage. After a few rough, split-lip, hole-busted-in-wall fights during adolescence, his older brother nick names him "bulldog." For any attack on his pride, he rushes head first into a fisticuffs. His eyes are round and shallow, with thick brows completing a wandering gaze. His nose sits broad and close to his face as if designed to resist the chill of Nordic winds. He works part-time at Henson Lumber Yard, mostly cutting and stacking large quantities of two-by-fours and half-inch plywood. One summer, the owner promotes him to drive a four-ton flatbed.

Barely nineteen, horsing around out in the hills on a motorcycle rigged for dirt trails, he tries to outmaneuver his younger brother, speeds down a ditch, and slams his skull against a cement clod, blood dripping from the gash in his forehead. He rests in bed for more than two weeks, brooding, mostly pouting, and recuperating from a concussion. One night, lying in bed, trying to fall asleep with the thumping in his head, he discovers the Rush

Limbaugh radio show and learns that Republicans eliminate taxes and Democrats increase them. He never forgets this idea. His busty girlfriend appears often at his bedroom isolated from the rest of the house, her comforting visits sealed the bond for a first marriage. He quits junior college and works full-time hauling building materials for Henson Lumber Co. Two years later he moves to Rogue River, Oregon, and starts driving an eighteen wheeler. The absent husband, on the road most of the time, learns about infidelities that end his marriage. But the scar on his forehead remains intact.

Barely twenty-three, Solumund takes a ride in his pickup skanking for a new beer bar and a new barfly to jack up in a no-tell motel down in Klamath Falls. Out on 9th and Main streets, he passes a little blond who is stopped on the roadside, pulling a spare tire out of her trunk. Six months later, he marries Hailey. Four months later, she is pregnant and Solumund is proud. His head and neck don't bother him much anymore. Hailey is a college graduate and becomes the brains of the family. A year younger than Solumund, she has an undistinguished, oval face, hair cut square at her shoulders. A little stout but she looks fine in the winter with large, wool sweaters.

Solumund's mother and father are happy that their son is settling down now, though he is on the road most of the time hauling goods along the west coast as far as Seattle and Los Angeles. He hitches onto the good money during the 1970s when the trucking business booms. Some singer named McCall does a song especially for truckers called *Convoy* that tops the billboard of hits. Solumund figures this is the best way to make a living. He doesn't have to sit in any class room learning from books and paying tuition. Miles and miles flow under his eighteen wheels, the hours pass as he rolls down Interstate 5, listening to country music or to Rush Limbaugh and hearing about some hostage situation and how President Carter asks Americans to reduce their consumption of gas. He listens about how Reagan should become president and how Reaganomics can reduce taxes and create prosperity by deregulation and less government. At home he talks to his father about the confusing world beyond the highway. His father balks and collects a jar full of soot off his old Ford pickup. From the Mt. St. Helen's volcanic eruption, it covers everything like a blanket of dark snow.

The federal government passes the Motor Carrier Act that deregulates the trucking industry, dramatically increasing the number of trucking companies in operation. Almost overnight Solumund's income is cut in half. One day he is part of a union and then the next day he says to Hailey, "Everyone is driving up and down the highway. Now there's nothing but towelheads haulin. I can't keep up. I gotta put in more hours to pay the mortgage."

Three months later, Solumund stops taking handfuls of the off-the-shelf no-doze tablets when a trucker buddy introduces him to Manuel who sells him a couple grams of quality Columbian cocaine. Now he can put in the hours and keep up the income. But his hankering for more of the blow seems to pull harder and harder at his sleeve every day. He has to buy more and more of it just to keep going. In less than a year, he's strung out, can't sleep much, and his night vision blurs. He can't afford to buy the clean coke but the cheaper stuff turns his head into a whining blender scramble. One night he dozes off and runs his semi into a highway sign. Two months later, he talks to himself while driving all night. His ghost is possessed by the snow. On one of the rare weekends when he rests at home, Hailey says, "You're working too much. It's turning you into a sniggering maniac."

Two months later he pulls into a truck stop to buy a gram of the white powder. Two young ladies walk up to the diner. He pulls open his overalls, giggles, and wags his pecker at them under the bright parking lot lights. Police cuff him. He faces a felony. The judge offers to go easy since he's a father and orders him to do rehab and community work for a year. Hailey is pregnant with twin boys. She and Solumund decide to move closer to his parents' place. They find a house outside Keno and Hailey's parents help them with a down payment.

Solumund tries to find a job repairing semis. With a record, finding a job is all uphill pushing. Unemployed, he is heavier and moodier. He works some odd jobs at a lumber mill at minimum wage. His father loans him all his tools and spends time with him, showing him how to fix the big rigs. Hailey's belly is ballooning with twins. They hear on the news about the Iran Contra Affair and how three of Reagan's cabinet members are pardoned for their felonies. He buys the utility truck from his father and rebuilds the engine.

The twins are born. Solumund starts taking his utility truck out on calls to repair semis broke down on the highway. The money is good but the calls are infrequent. Hailey is good at keeping the books. Solumund learns on the news that there's some twenty million trucks on the road now. With all those trucks, they figure the truckers will be glad to get their rigs repaired at a convenient spot between Redding and Portland. They start a business. Hailey gets business cards printed up. They spruce up the old barn and turn it into a repair shop. It's just big enough to fit a big diesel Freightliner tractor inside. His father's hair falls out and he can't walk as strong as he once did. His father likes to tell the joke, "Old truckers never die, they just get a new Peterbuilt." The old man might have cancer. Doctor says two, three years. He likes to roll his own cigarettes with fresh tobacco, an old habit from the farm days in South Dakota. Shrapnel finally works its way to the top layers of his skin, so he goes to the veteran's hospital to have it removed. He says, "The nurse looked to see if I had any of that strong German metal in my thighs." He wears a baseball cap that reads, "Live long. It's the best revenge."

A great mother, Hailey takes their daughter to all the 4-H Club meetings. Their daughter presents a lamb. Four years later, she wins a prize for her black Angus, which they sell for $900—though the costs of raising the beast are as much. Solumund says, “Yeah, well, think of it as the price of an education in the real world and leave it at that.” The twins grow up. Both are mechanically inclined and maybe have an aptitude for engineering. Both are athletic and occasionally win long-distance bicycle races.

Hailey drives a school bus on the side to add some income. She’s not much of a cook, even though she studied nutrition and home economics. She tends to spend everything she makes on junk food. She gains weight. Solumund’s mother says to him, “She’s beginning to resemble that 100-gallon tank of diesel out behind your shop.” He turns his head and escapes out to the barn where a Freightliner waits for new brakes.

The kids grow tall. The daughter marries a young man, apparently from a wealthy family. They move to Louisiana, in some town with a French name that Solumund can’t pronounce. Five years later, the young couple moves back near Klamath Falls and looks for work. Hailey and Solumund refinance their property. They use the cash equity to help the young couple start a FedEx service in Siskiyou County. Solumund gets extra work repairing the delivery trucks.

A bad year hits. Worried about Jens, Solumund's mother calls him saying, "He didn't come home for lunch." Solumund drives around searching for his father and finds him at the first place he looks: down at the coffee shop, where the old man always talks with his buddies. He sees his dad sitting in his beat-up Ford pickup in parking lot, his eyes fixed out the windshield at the sunset. Solumund opens the driver's door. His dad sits there motionless. Solumund breaks down and cries for the first time in his adult life. His brothers and sister attend the early morning funeral. They sit together for the first time in decades and have a pizza at lunch time, and then start their long drives back to their homes out of state.

Three months later, Hailey's hips give out after several operations. She can no longer walk and uses an electric cart, specially designed for her weight, to get around the house.

Despite their expensive health insurance, Solumund has to pay for the extra medical services. He has to refinance the property again. He spends more and more time in his shop, making up for the bills. The winter is especially cold and arthritis in his neck forces him to take painkillers. The radio in his shop tells him that Operation Iraqi Freedom is a farce based on lies. These days he has no time to listen to Rush Limbaugh. He hears about the financial collapse on Wall Street and how taxpayers have to clean up the mess. He sets his radio to country western music and goes about his business.

Stay Frosty

They had trained together at Fort Irwin Army base in the Mojave Desert. Young then, they had lost touch over the years. It looked like Kris Klug had a reason to contact him now. Bill Greco had paid those years at the Wasco Prison, Bakersfield, California, for conspiracy to blow up a family planning clinic in Venice, California. His time inside the no-tail motel fortified his religious fervor and gave him a purpose.

Through his battle buddy network, Klug had heard stories how Greco had received his ordination as Divine Deacon from the Theology Academy of Lake Forest, Orange County. Once back outside in the world, Greco formed a congregation with the guys he had met on the inside and with others from the local churches who'd bathed in the light. He called his group Christ's Warriors and held regular meetings at an old place in the hills just east of Laguna Beach, where he preached to his group of fervent believers about God's path and purpose in life. He took his cue from the extremely popular and prosperous Rick Warhand, who had captured the zeitgeist of America and put it in a book, guiding the aimless wonderers onto a purposeful trail to God's truth.

What he did next, Greco got to know Warhand, a man he'd read about as an influential mover and shaker in the spheres of the Family. He'd met the famous man personally, shook his hand at his mega-church in Irvine, seeking advice on spiritual leadership for his newly gathered prayer group, a bunch of boys wearing faded blue jeans and leather vests, scruffy beards and shaved heads mostly. Well-trained Marines and Army grunts who had a home in their new family of the faithful, rebels against overbearing government and taxes and anything un-American, but still had to be taught how to follow what Greco called the righteous laws as laid out in the Lord's own words, ones he'd learned about from Chuck's Prison Fellowship, a worldwide Christian powerhouse that had declared civil war on secularism and senators voting for healthcare. Word was out that even G. W. Bush had found his purpose this way while he struggled through alcohol's darkness and failures as a Texas oil man.

He trained these boys to ensure that the Lord's rules were followed in this great chosen land of freedom and prosperity. "Enforcing the laws," he said in one of his sermons, "requires more than prayers and faith. And, yeah, you bet, reasonable use of explosives, in the right places, and weapons, and skill in generating income by commerce with the other races, especially those south of the border." He felt strengthened when he read about Democratic Congressman Mike McIntyre's belief that the Ten Commandments should be the fundamental legal code of the United States.

Once sworn to take up the crusade for Christ in preparation for the Rapture, Greco personally certified his band of brothers. In one of his speeches, Greco said their next job was to do some business in Mexicali. They needed regular revenue to operate and get back on their feet after incarceration.

The boys took Greco's word as gospel, just as they did for Pastor Warhand. They bonded tightly as a unit under Greco, revering him as a warrior who faced raw combat for years in Afghanistan and Iraq. He had served as a Ranger and came back with the tattoos to announce it, plus five golden rings that he'd pulled off the fingers of Republican Guard officers he'd put down.

A few years younger than Greco, Kris Klug had taken over his uncle's trucking business, hauling goods from Los Angeles to Las Vegas Casinos. Among Klug's small circle of old battle buddies he was known as one of the finest Green Berets, a team leader in Operation Iraqi Freedom and one of the first in for the Anaconda operation. Klug was the one who had picked apart a six-man drug ring practically single handedly when the gang chased him and a handful of clueless civilians across the Mojave Desert. He helped a group of terrorized city dwellers escape from cold-blooded killers. Once he found a Winchester rifle in an old miner's hideaway, he turned the odds against the well-armed criminals, picking off each of them whenever the Mojave winds and whims presented the opportunity.

Klug was managing his trucking business when his wife, Sheila, witnessed the kidnapping of one of her best friends. Sheila saw four big scruffy men in a white van that slowed down and nabbed her friend while crossing Las Vegas Boulevard—on the famous Vegas strip.

That same day Greco headed south of the border with his gang to do another transaction. He was leading his small pack in an old Ford Escape covered in mud and dust so thick the plates were concealed coming out of the dirt roads west of the 405 Freeway. The car belonged to his new recruit, Hound, a middle-aged guy from the eastern hills of Southern California who'd shaved his head and face clean and just completed Greco's three-month indoctrination to become a brother in the group. Greco turned to Hound, saying, "You heard about how the Mongol's shot a CHP right here on this patch of highway, not a week ago?"

"Shoot a cop," Hound said, his hands on the wheel, eyes down the road, a view of cars and semis. He said, "Stupid ass idea, shoot a CHP off his bike on the freeway. Why not hit the whole damn station with a bomb? Better yet, pop an RPG at the IRS building, rattle their computer screens. Shake them up."

Sounded tough enough, but did he have the balls for it? This old boy, Hound, from Temecula, talked big, but acted more like an ass-dragging yahoo.

Three hours ago they had come out of a run-down house hidden in the hills around the Laguna Beach area. Now they were turning off Highway 5 onto Highway 80, heading east, bypassing San Diego, packing their protection. Hidden in the trunk's spare tire hole were a couple of AK47s with plenty of ammo, the weapon Greco had learned to love once he'd pulled one off a Republican Guard fighter.

"Think about what you learned during training. Anything unclear?" He asked Hound.

The sun was setting as they pulled up next to an 18-wheeler. Hound shrugged his shoulders, speeding up a little to pass it. He played the confident, lazy tough guy, raising his eyebrows as if surprised there would be anything not to understand, and then paused before saying, "Well, there is maybe one thing. Why the hell we doing business with Mexicans if they are subhuman?"

"Oh, hell," Greco said. "You need to read up on the Bible. What the hell you do with your time up there in Wasco? Like you remember not a damn thing."

"Yeah, well," said Hound, "you're younger, smarter. I did not have all the advantages you did."

That was why they called him Hound, dumb as a dog, or maybe he just played his hand that way. He landed in Wasco six months before Greco's release and paid only six months for a parole violation—carrying a weapon in this very same car, the old Ford Escape. Or maybe the heat was just planted there so Hound could break into Greco's little group.

Hound claimed he was anxious to join Greco's prayer group, learn a purpose for his life instead of peddling pot and stealing cars. Shit, Hound told how he had caught the tail end of Vietnam, come back with two gunshot scars on his shoulder and chest, wounds that won him a Purple Heart. Said he was in New York City just after the disaster, volunteered to help clean up the rubble. He said he was inspired to serve a higher calling. Getting into the fight against the nonbelievers seemed to give meaning to his time in Vietnam, more than anything else since.

This Hound guy from Temecula—Greco and the others were not convinced he was everything he said he was. Why no tattoos from Nam, no colorful dragons, nothing? Why always clean shaved? Greco did not like it much, made Hound look like a skinhead. He did not fit in. Greco's boys were followers of Jesus, but they didn't like the term Christian. Instead they followed Pat Roberston's Jesus, a personal Christ, with a purpose, unlike those skinheads—God-damned anarchists. No, Greco preferred the regulation Army cut. It felt comfortable. In his late fifties, Hound could not shave close enough to hide the gray stubble that dusted his head and face, leathery from too much sun.

They had long since passed San Diego, speeding straight south of Vegas. Approaching the border now, Hound pointed out the lights of Mexicali, and remarked how they sparkled in the desert.

"Our meeting point is ten miles passed the border," said Greco. "Take the Barranca exit. Bullet and Spider are supposed to be there right now with the merchandise."

"Another thing," said Hound, "those other clubs, they're already established and making good money. Why don't we just join? We could do a franchise with the HAs.
They make loads of money."

"Except," said Greco, "they don't follow Jesus. We're different, you know why?"

Silence fell and then Hound said, "Is that the turnoff here?"

"Ten miles I said. We've only done five. And the God-damned question?"

Hound paused, fumbled to light a cigarette while keeping a hand on the wheel. "Jesus Christ, man, what question?"

"Exactly right," he said. "We got purpose with J.C. Them other bikers, Hell's Angels, Mongols, Outlaws, Skulls, all they do—they make money. They aren't right with God."

They were at the turnoff now passing that big billboard advertising Zapatista Tequila.

"Here's the exit. They should be another mile down this path." He pointed at a dirt road barely visible in the sandy desert.

Greco took in the terrain. "You got millions and millions in the States who go through life without a clue. Watching TV all night. Zombies is what they are, the real felons in this whole mess. They hide from the invasion, Mexicans going north. Just look around here, this city Mexicali, anarchy and chaos, what it is. No control over their police and military. They need to hire a private militia, kick ass."

He paused to tell Hound where to go but he had already spotted the others, four young men standing around smoking cigarettes waiting for action. Hound just drove up to them.

"Stay put," he said, "keep the engine idle. We'll be out a here in five."

Greco walked over to his other four recruits, skinny guys in their early twenties. He'd indoctrinated them while at Wasco. Kids wandering aimlessly without a compass until he'd broke them down to become followers of the Lord Savior.

They had parked a couple hundred yards behind the billboard. All you could see for miles around was flat sand dotted with cactus, sagebrush, and yuccas.

His operations man, Gypsy, had explained to him that the four kids had picked up a dancer on their way through Vegas. Just like Greco planned it. The HA had put a contract on her. The tall, slim dancer worked the grand venues, the MGM, Paris, and Alladin. Gypsy told Greco what the HA had told him—the story how she had gone out dating one of the highest ranking Hell's Angels and ran off with a couple pounds of pot. When the HA asked her to return it, she threatened to call the police. What she did was criminal. Gypsy said she was a felon.

Greco looked in the back door of the kids' van reeled from the thick cloud of pot smoke. The young recruits hadn't bothered to open even a window as they made their way south. One of the four kids, Sidney, said, "We snatched her off the sidewalk, quick and smooth just like Gypsy told us to do."

Through the haze Greco spotted a teenage girl. "Who the hell is she?"

"They were walking together," said Bullet, "hand in hand like mother and daughter. Sidney here, he wanted a piece of her, but I told him we should wait for you, maybe you wanted first dibs."

"Don't you even think of it," he said dead serious. "We sell them to Torrez for the dope and we're out of here. Get this livestock across the border before anyone sees our footprints. You hear me?"

"That's a gyp," Gypsy said. "We did all the work. We got the dancer here, plus this bonus princess. We ball her a little, Torrez won't even know about it. He'll pay the same price in pounds of dope."

Bullet shrugged and snorted, then spit a wad of tobacco.

Gary, the youngest of the four said, "Hell yeah, we got time. Take turns with both."

"Shut up," said Hog, who sat behind the wheel. "You deaf?"

Greco heard the noise of car wheels on the gravel road, turned around, and said, "They're here. Now keep shut, I do the talking."

Two black SUVs pulled up with their windows rolled down behind the white van, with four Mexicans each one. Only Torrez opened his door and stepped out. "You bring merchandise?"

"The dancer," said Greco and gestured to the kids in the van to pull the woman out.

They held her, standing up outside the van. "You got the payment?"

Torrez went to the open window in the back of the second SUV and pulled out a leather bag and handed it to Greco, who rifled through the contents, pinched some of the white powder, and dabbed a bit on his tongue. He then motioned to Hog and Sidney to hand the woman over to Torrez.

She tried to struggle and to scream but the duct tape held her hands, ankles, and lips. They shoved her quickly into the cargo area of the second SUV.

“Got more of this?” Greco said, holding up the leather bag.

“You got more womans, my man?” Torrez asked.

“Got any more powder?” he said.

“We can bring some,” said Torrez. “What you got?”

“When can you bring more powder?” he asked.

“Tomorrow, noon.” Torrez looked back at the SUV where his men held the younger woman.

“Let’s set up another meeting when you have it ready,” Greco said.

Torrez returned to the SUV and both black vehicles disappeared into the night.

Gypsy stood by the side of the van, hands in his pocket. “What do we do with the extra chick?”

“She’s our new girlfriend,” said Bullet as all four jumped into the van. Hog was behind the wheel starting the engine, his window open where Greco leaned in and barked his commands. “No one touches her. We take her back north to the church. We wait for

Torrez to come up with the next bag of snow." He banged his hand a couple times on the window frame and door to make sure everyone understood he meant business. "Torrez doesn't come through, me and Gypsy'll find a buyer." He walked back to Hound's Ford Escape and sat quickly in the back seat, just behind Hound.

The four kids drove away in their van, heading north.

'What you want to do? Drive back with them?" Hound said, watching.

"No, let's just wait here a minute," he said, "Let them take a lead."

Hound stayed behind the wheel when Greco jumped out of the Ford with his cell phone to his ear, trying to call Gypsy to announce the change in plans. No answer. So he left a voice message saying something clever and cryptic since he never trusted phones, especially now with the phone-tapping Feds. He said something about how they'd picked a bundle of virgin wool for the trip back north, and we needed to locate a buyer.

Gypsy was the one who first drove down to Mexicali to do what he called establishing a relationship with Torrez and his crew so as to have a supplier for some of the purest grade cocaine on the market. Only thing was, he came back with three teenage senoritas he sold to some pimp in the east side who ran a little Latin Spice Spa in the Silver Lake area. They made a good fifteen grand off the deal but one of the girls had heard Greco's name in one of the conversations during negotiations in Mexicali.

The girl mentioned the name to her clients like Greco was the owner of the spa. It became just one more nagging note in Greco's police file. They could've robbed a Mexican bank and spray-painted "Greco's Group" on the wall—same results, except you get away with a bundle of cash, a lot more than ten grand.

It was Gypsy who told him to watch out for Hound—both Gypsy and Greco's little brother, Spider, figured Hound was an ATF agent or some such thing, the only way to explain why he played so damn dumb.

Greco got back into the Ford and Hound said, "Where to?"

"Back on the 22, south." Greco sat in the back seat not making a sound.

Fifteen miles farther south, Greco said, "Next turn up here to the right." Another half mile, Greco could see the lights on down the gravel road. "We're coming to it," he said, looking at the stone fence all lit up with spot lights like some sort of high-roller estate. Hound stopped the car where Greco told him to pull over on the side of the long driveway in the dark.

Gypsy told him about the place. "Torrez's ranch."

"Huge place," said Hound, eyes focused straight ahead, "for a rancher."

"What they call a hacienda, except he hardly has any livestock," he said. "Not since he got into the business."

"Why we sittin here?" Hound said, still facing forward.

"I come here just to see," he said. "Now that I'm here, I'd like to lob a grenade on his house. Payback for not buying that second girl."

"Greco, there's guards standing around that entrance gate. You can see them under that bright light. They'll see my car, we sit here long enough.

Greco lived for moments like this. He could show his combat toughness. "Worried they might spot us out here, huh?"

Could be this Hound was a snitch like Gypsy and Spider suspected. One thing was sure, for his age and experience, he was not warrior class.

"How come you play so dumb all the time?" he said, pulling out his red bandana from his back pocket which he normally tied around his forehead when he was engaging in action.

"Like to ask questions, is all."

"How'd you know where to turn off the highway into Torrez's place here?"

Greco barely had to lean over to grab Hound's 9mm Glock he kept under his driver's seat. "I'd say you like to ask more questions than you wanna explain."

Hound raised his eyes to the rearview mirror. "You stayed in your seat back there during the whole transaction like you didn't want any part of it."

"Yeah, you told me to stay, keep the engine running."

Hound sounded like he was going to panic again. Greco wondered a second to himself. You want to get this done, or sit here and chat.

He pulled the pistol up behind Hound's head rest and, bam, shot Hound through the back of the neck. The bullet tore flesh, with blood splattering the windshield, and left a hole in the glass.

He pulled Hound's body out of the driver's seat, left it there in a ditch on the side of the road, used his bandanna to wipe off the windshield, and sped away in the night.

Only after he'd gone back to Mexicali, heading northeast on the 80 toward the border, that Gypsy finally returned his call.

Gypsy wanted to talk on the phone, but Greco just said, "Left the hound with the rancher, he can take care of it. Let's talk when I get back."

Into Mexicali now, on Oaxaca Street, Greco had parked Hound's car only a couple miles from a bus station. He had to wait only a half hour for the next one to San Diego. He'd textmessaged Gypsy to pick him up.

During the drive back to their little warehouse in the Laguna Beach area, Greco filled him in: how they'd traded the dancer from

Vegas for the blow as agreed—Gypsy high-fiving to celebrate the deal done—and then how Torrez had backed out of taking on the girl and how he'd left Hound for Torrez. He figured it served that rancher right for not taking the girl off their hands for a fair price.

Greco licked a zig-zag cigarette page and pasted it to a second one, pulled a little pouch out of the glove box of Gypsy's old Chevy pickup, sprinkled marijuana into the fold of paper and rolled it to light it. He looked over at Gypsy's shaved head and face and Army-green cap and passed the joint over to him.

"Cut the edge off a day like today," he said.

"I hear ya," said Gypsy.

"Did you tell Hound how to find Torrez's place?" he said.

"Yep," said Gypsy, puffing the smoke

"Why?"

"He asked," said Gypsy, passing the joint back to him. "Look, it's done, the damn snitch."

They arrived close enough now to see the light on the front porch of Greco's old church. It was an old building he had inherited when his grandmother died while he was still at Wasco. One of the older buildings in the area, it perched on the side of one of the many hills that separated the town of Laguna Beach from the 405 Highway. His grandmother had transformed the backend of the old church into a little house, nestled at the foot of the hill where his grandfather repaired cars for a living in a small barn. They passed the PRIVATE PROPERTY—STAY THE HELL OUT sign that Greco put up first day he moved into the place.

All four of what he called the kids—Sidney, Bullet, Gary, and Spider—were sitting on the back porch watching him and Gypsy walking up to the house.

Greco said, "What's wrong with you?" to his brother Spider, who held an icepack on his head.

It was Bullet who finally spoke up. "Spider here got a little too close to the girl, trying to take her pants off, check things out, when she gave him a mule's kick square in the cahunas. He bent over, feeling the pain when she punted his nose. But it was him falling backwards on his own awkward feet made him bounce his skull on the kitchen table that knocked him out a minute or two."

"What about the girl?" Greco asked, unconcerned about his little brother.

"She's fine," said Sidney. "Let her alone in the kitchen, cooling off."

"We kept an eye on her," said Bullet, "real wild one."

"Spider learned the hard way how you gotta bring flowers, get a girl's pants off," said Bullet, muffling his chuckles.

It was Sheila, Kris Klug's wife, who called that afternoon when three guys jumped out of a white van and grabbed her friend Karla and her daughter, Sara. The two women and Sara, just a teenager, were so shocked they didn't have time to react, Sheila explained to Kris. "They just grabbed, Karla—two men, snatched her up, carried her to the van, and flung her in like a sack of potatoes, and the third guy threw Sara across his shoulders. She went kicking and screaming. A couple of them came back, running for me, but I ran into a coffee shop on the corner, locked myself in the bathroom."

"What'd they look like?" said Kris.

"Three young, skinny guys like in their twenties, all wearing baseball caps down over their faces. One had a tattoo on his neck, like two lightning bolts."

"How long ago?" he asked.

"Minutes ago, I'm still locked in the bathroom. I didn't know what to do."

"Where are you?"

"That coffee shop down on the strip. You know the one," she said.

"Be there in a couple minutes," said Klug, who started sprinting to the old jeep his uncle had left him.

When he reached the coffee shop Sheila came outside and gave him a hug so solid it reminded him of when they had first met in a dangerous predicament.

"Let's get you home," he said. "I'll make you a chamomile tea, calm your nerves." He had already helped her up to her seat, buckled her seatbelt, and started heading back.

"Sounds good," she said, folding her arms.

"Set you up with a nice warm bubble bath."

"Perfect," she said, leaning her head on his shoulder. "We should call the police."

"I already did," he said, "on the way to picking you up. I'll talk with them once I get you settled down."

"You should go," she said. "They got Karla and her daughter. What can the police do to catch them?"

"I'll go in," he said. "The police have to get on the case and follow the threads nonstop until they finish it. The first hours are crucial."

***

Xavier Chavez was in charge of Las Vegas Special detachment for abductions. He had already asked one of his staff to get Kris Klug in the office with his wife, Sheila, since she was a witness. Klug was seated in Chavez's temporary office in the Vegas County courthouse.

It was the usual bright, blue sky day in the desert, even though it was mid-September. The two sipped iced tea, getting acquainted again.

“Normally, a situation like this, we’d have officers out searching,” said Chavez.

“Well, then, why aren’t we doing just that?”

“We already found video of the white van at the border crossing at Mexicali. We searched the area. Contacted the Mexican Federales, as usual they say they’ll keep an eye out. We didn’t find the van but we did find a Ford Escape crossing the border last night, belongs to a Joseph David, a.k.a. Hound. Guy’s still on parole, out on a felony. He first came out of Wasco couple months ago. His file says when he was in Wasco he joined a small religious group led by a lowlife called Greco, some kind of Christian Prison Fellowship.”

“So, you know who did this?” said Kris.

“You know the rules,” said Chavez. “Until we have solid evidence we got squat.”

“The good news,” said Kris. “Tell me a good thing.”

“We have their trail,” said Chavez. “MLS—they headed for Mexicali to sell the women. It’s a routine business now a days. Most likely left the woman, Karla, and her daughter down there. Most likely your friend Karla did something to piss them off. Normally, this sort of thing is done in revenge.”

"What the hell's MLS mean?"

"Most likely scenario," said Chavez.

"Why?" said Kris.

"You read the papers, don't you?"

"What about it?" he said, finishing his glass of iced tea quickly. "Most likely scenario?"

"They take the women as payment for drugs," said Chavez. "Most likely, that Greco dude already put together a little gang and barters the women for dope to sell here. The two women are down there. Right out of the stir, he's short on cash."

"So, go find them," he said, crossing one leg over a knee, his hand on his boot.

"Not our jurisdiction," said Chavez. "And I didn't tell you this but the Federales never cooperate with us. My boss here doesn't like me saying things like that to our taxpayers, but, hell, I don't consider you a civilian, bud."

"How many?" he said.

"What we can do is look for Greco and whatever cargo his little team brought back up here, if my theory's right."

"You didn't answer my question." He let his boot back down square on the tile floor with a thud.

"No, but did I need to?" said Chavez. "You know the score. Why you so tied to this anyway? Your wife is safe."

"The woman, Karla," he said, "she's one of my wife's best friends. Maybe she doesn't have good judgment in the men in her life, but my wife's been working with her for years and almost got snatched up with them."

"I understand," said Chavez, "but you've done enough now. Your wife gave me all she knows. What more can you do?"

"And the girl?" He raised his voice. "We have to do something. What happens to her? Get sold into some sex slave ring?"

"Look," said Chavez, "I've told you all I know for now. I'll keep you informed."

"Yeah," he said, "you gotta follow the rules."

"M?" Chavez said, calling Klug by his military nickname.

"You know damned well," he said.

"You're going south?" Chavez said.

"I'll make it my jurisdiction."

“Damn it,” said Chavez, “why get so involved. You’ve already done plenty. You know what kind of shit’s going on down there? The friggin Mexican Army and the Police are taking commissions off the drug deals. The drug lords have taken over most of the country. Hell, half the time, the Army and police are nothing but security guards for one drug lord or another. Just like it was in that screwed up Afghanistan. Cuttin heads off ‘n all that shit. I don’t have to explain it.”

“For my wife,” he said.

“Simple as that, huh?” Chavez said, “How the hell are you anyway?”

“What you mean?” he said.

“We haven’t had a beer together since you got all that TV coverage as the Green Beret put out that little band of hajji gangsters in the Mojave.”

“I really didn’t need all that attention,” he said. “All kinds of goofballs came looking around for interviews, snapshots, like I was part of the tourist scenery.”

“That was a couple years ago.”

“Yeah,” he said. “Thank God people have moved on, forgot the whole damn thing.”

“You haven’t changed much, still the go-getter like back at the farm,” said Chavez, meaning the time they both trained together at Fort Bragg in North Carolina getting their Spec Ops qualification. “Still wearing those heavy boots?”

“Practically new ones, this pair. Need to break’em in.”

“What about that fatigue hat?” said Chavez. “I bet it’s the same you wore back at the farm.”

It was Klug’s idea of keeping a low profile. He thought of it as a fishing hat, except that it was an Army cap and there was hardly any fishing holes in the desert—unless you paid for it—this thread-bare one with its small hole, flopped down over his eyebrows so you wouldn’t know who its owner was. Part of his disguise as some hard-luck concrete handler out looking for work.

“And I bet you still pack one under your shirt,” said Chavez.

“The reliable one,” he said.

“What?” said Chavez. “That old 45 service pistol they gave us? You still carry that thing around?”

“Only on special occasions, like this,” he said.

"You're serious about this, aren't you?"

"I told you. It's some of my wife's best friends," said Klug.

"Must be one kind of special wife you got there."

"Weren't for her, I'd be a pile of baked bones in that Mojave. She's the one pulled me out of a stupor."

"Well," said Chavez, "you and me always been on the same side of the fight. I'm with you, bro. You know it. I gotta stay in the frame of this job. Only thing pays my mortgage."

Silence settled between the two veterans. Klug looked out the window at the clear skies and the traffic zipping by Gold Dust Boulevard in Vegas.

A medium sized man, comfortable in his skin but energetic, soft spoken, Chavez said, "Tell me whatever you remember of Greco."

Klug, nodding his head, commanded his mind to go back in time. "We started training at Fort Irwin together. He came from some small town, Wayne, Nebraska, I think. Said his father disappeared in Nam, his mother and grandma raised him, lived in some mobile home place, northeast corner of Nebraska, practically the wilderness. He wanted to follow his father's footsteps, you know, join that Army of One. He was frustrated not getting into Spec Ops but settled for Ranger. Couple years older 'n me. We went through sniper school in dead summer, frying our butts off, working out desert camouflage details. 'Stay frosty,' he'd say all the time, always a joker."

Chavez raised his eyebrows. "'Stay frosty,' huh?"

"Damn good marksman," he said. "Better than me, at the time anyway." He winked at Chavez as if to say, not any more.

"We were put together on a mission in Iraq once, worked with him a few days over there. A couple weeks later I heard he pleaded guilty during a special court-martial. He was busted in rank to private E-2, made to forfeit his salary for three months, and sent off on the worst night raids I ever heard of."

"Well," said Chavez, "you two have at least special court-martial in common."

"The fuck that mean?" he said.

"What he get busted for?" said Chavez.

"I heard, he wore the ears of the Republican Guard officers he'd killed, cut them off, dried them out in the sun and strung them on his dog-tags chain, wore 'em like a trophy. His CO busted him for carrying cocaine, stuff to keep him alert during the night mission. I'm not sure what to believe. You got his file, right?"

"Only his criminal rap," said Chavez. "Cops don't have access to military records. I did call and poke around the paper pushers in Maryland, and one of those office toads told me Greco worked odd jobs along the eastern seaboard, mostly construction. He applied for a job with the CIA, probably figured as a busted Army Ranger, the spooks would be eager. He came to California and started making good money running cocaine from Mexico. Got busted. Did his time."

"And now here he is, huh, right back at it?" he said.

"Only thing is," said Chavez, "he learned religion in Wasco, now he's got a team of fools following him. I figure he don't have much money to start up another operation so he's selling women south of the border, beauties like this Karla and her daughter fetch premium prices down there."

"Yeah, he was into one of those Bible thumping churches on the base in Iraq, too," said Klug. "Anyway, Karla had a bonus on her head. She had a short romance with a guy who was reselling for some Mexican, and when she found out, she snitched."

"Yeah," said Chavez, "your wife explained as much over the phone."

"So," he said, "you know the Mexican's name?"

"I've been tracking it down," said Chavez. "Her boyfriend's name is Olson." He shuffled through a folder of papers. "Dart…Dart Olson, and I'm working on finding out that his supplier was in Mexico. Someone at the FBI mentioned a guy named Torrez down in Mexicali."

"You got the guy, what was it? Hound? You got Greco with Hound?"

"No. All we know—and again, I didn't tell you anything—Hound's car was registered in Temecula," said Chavez. "We think Greco is working somewhere in southern California. We don't have Greco with Hound yet, but we know for certain they were Bible brothers at Wasco."

"I vaguely remember Greco saying something about a brother somewhere around San Diego, but that was years ago," he said, standing up and adjusting his hat.

"I'll run a search on that," said Chavez. "Who knows what name he uses."

“No clue,” he said, walking out the door before Chavez could ask where he was going.

Heading straight south to Mexicali, he didn’t blink before he knew his plan. Simple enough: look for Hound and Greco and the others in this group, white van, like finding a needle in a haystack. Torrez should be easier to find.

A couple hours later he crossed into Mexicali, following Highway 111, down the west side of the city, and stopped at the first dingy truck stop he could find and took a seat at the bar, a place Chavez mentioned to him as one of Torrez’s hangouts.

Two riders from a local ranch—its name, El Mulito, branded into the back of their denim jackets like they belonged to some motorcycle club—were at a table with bottles of beer. One was an old boy, with weathered skin, the other a young buck who wore a sweat-stained hat over his eyes as they both stared at Klug and he, in turn, kept an eye on them through the mirror behind the bar.

Right there, not a minute later the bartender poured him a second shot of Zapatista Tequila, talking to him as he washed it down. The two rancheros were still staring at his back like they’d never seen a gringo in that bar, its name in big red letters above the mirror: El Gaucho.

The young one asked the older, "*¿Has visto un gringo mas feo*?"

Klug, calculating how to make this work on his terms, asked the bartender, "*¿De donde vienen los dos Zapatistas*?"

The bartender didn't answer, but when they finished their beers, the two men walked up to the bar.

The bartender appeared to smile, for some reason finding humor in Klug's question.

"*Que quieres aqui?*" the old ranchero asked.

"*Ponder*," said Klug, looking straight ahead into the mirror.

"Powder," said the old ranchero in English.

"White powder," said Klug.

The young cowboy pulled out a tiny plastic bag from his pocket and dropped it on the bar, saying, "*cien dolares.*"

"*Necesito un kilo, pura*," said Klug.

The younger one squinted beneath his hat funneled low on his eyes. "*Es posible, pero necesito diez mil dolares cash.*"

Klug pulled a wad of cash from his jacket and flashed it.

"*Regresamos en 30 minutos*," said the older one.

Kris nodded.

The two rancheros left in a new Ford pickup, promising to bring back a kilo of pure snow for a cool ten grand.

Kris waited a couple of minutes and hopped in this jeep, following them at a distance, his lights turned off.

Not five miles down the road, the rancheros turned onto a gravel road.

Klug parked his jeep off the road a few yards away from the gravel driveway and walked a couple yards off the side, moving toward the lights of the ranch house a couple hundred yards into the desert from the road.

Hardly had he taken forty paces, he saw a pack of coyotes chewing their way through the carcass of a clothed human body.

He tossed a couple rocks at the coyotes and approached for a closer look. The face of a middle-aged white man, his head barely attached, his body torn by the hungry animals. With the tip of his boot he pushed the body over and found the man's wallet among the remains of his torn trousers. The wallet in his hands, he walked away, rifling through cards to find the name.

“This is too easy,” he whispered to himself and kept walking toward the area where he had seen the two rancheros park their pickups, its shiney new paint reflecting in its brake-lights. “Like this is the only supplier in the area.”

He lay flat on the ground waiting, watching with a pair of night vision binoculars.

Adjusting his sky glasses he saw four men talking in a room near the main entrance. Wondering if this was the right place where they sold Karla and her daughter, he slipped around to the side of the house but most of the windows were covered with blinds.

Then the two rancheros from the bar quickly marched to the pickup trucks with two more men.

One man carried a gym bag. All four men hopped into the Ford and sped off.

Now he moved in closer to the house, peering into the windows. One window was open wide, covered only by blinds. He moved from one window to another, checking, hoping to see Karla.

Passing through the only open window he found, he carefully moved from one room to the next. Silently and in the dark, he moved up the stairs and saw a bearded old man sitting in a chair outside a door.

When the man saw him approaching he began to say something in Spanish but didn't finish his sentence before Klug grabbed him by the throat from behind his chair. The guard struggle, his body twisted, and he groaned despite Klug's crushing grip over his Adam's apple. The man collapsed, dead.

The door to the room had been locked from the outside. After losing his assault knife trying to pry open the lock, he noticed the hinge pins, pried them out, and silently lifted the wooden door from its frame. Despite the room's darkness, light seeped in from the hall. He saw two beds in the small room, one woman lay flat, apparently sleeping, another sat up awake, eyes wide open, breathing deeply, gasping in fear of the man who entered the dark room. With the light at his back, he recognized Karla, and said, "It's me, Kris. Karla?"

She jumped up out of bed and hugged him tight, as if he was her only way out of hell. Her clothes were torn and a chain around her ankle kept her from moving any more than to a sink and toilet at the back of the room.

"Stay quiet," he whispered to her. "We'll get out."

He found the other end of the chain wrapped around the bed leg. He tried to lift the bed to free the chain but it was made of heavy wood and old ironwork. He crouched down, his back against the foot of the bed, and heaved with the force of his legs, clearing the bed leg from the old tile floor by hardly an inch, enough so she could pull the chain free.

"We have to get out of here," he whispered.

"What about her?" Karla pointed to the young woman chained to the other bed.

He tried shaking her to wake up. She didn't move. He held her wrist, looking for her pulse, nothing. He showed Karla the needle marks in the woman's arm. Putting his ear next to her nose and mouth, he felt no breath.

"She might be dead," he said.

Karla shrieked.

Klug took Karla's hand and headed for the door. "Let's go."

No sooner did they exit the back door of the house than a man stepped out of a big pickup truck, hair dyed blond, hanging long and straight over his shoulders, his shirt unbuttoned, revealing a tattoo across his chest, an image of Christ nailed to the cross. A tattoo of a rope around his neck sent the message that he belonged to the Mongols motorcycle club. "What you doing with the woman?" he said in Spanish.

"Who's asking," said Klug, in Spanish, ready to draw from his holster if it came to that.

Klug decided not to mess with Jesus Christ and asked, "So that's it, huh? You're riding with the Mongols or did you pick out the tat at the corner shop in town?"

This got the Mexican Mongol to squint at him even in the dark morning hour. He paused and then answered in English, "No ink shop nowhere round here."

"That right?" Klug raised his arm to scratch his head and showed the Green Beret logo tattooed on the underside of his arm. "You mind telling me your name?"

The Mexican Mongol was staring now as the sun was coming up, like he did mind and took time to answer.

Klug said, "You got a name?"

"Martin Torrez," the Mongol said, putting some grit into the sound of it.

"Carlos Torrez, my father, owner of this hacienda and you steal his property."

"Man," said Klug, "that's a hell of a father you got, thinks he can own people."

"Go back to norte," said Martin, "no business here for you."

"Well, now," said Klug "that would be my business to know. What is it exactly you and your father do?"

"I come to take this woman some place."

"That won't happen," said Klug.

"We paid for her." Martin took a step closer.

Klug held up his hand and it stopped the man's talk.

"I tell you what, Martin, no one buys anyone. This woman here, her name is Karla, a friend of mine. You are confused, made a bad purchase. Complain to your supplier, not to me."

Klug studied Martin's face, curious as to how this Mongol would take it, a big Mexican, more Spanish than Indian, a landowner, no apparent weapon on him.

"Lemme tell you," said Klug, "you go into your house there. You gotta woman chained to a bed. You gotta dead guard lying on the floor in front of the room where you keep women locked up. You go in and take care of the bodies. When you're done with that, well, by that time, Federales will be here to ask you why you think you can buy and sell women like cattle."

Martin said, "You in danger, my man, I tell you what."

Keeping it simple, gaining time, Martin said, "I'm gonna walk back to my truck and leave tha damn mess to mi padre. He make it, he clean up." He turned and headed back toward his big pickup.

Klug gestured for Karla to run down the driveway to his jeep, now visible in the first rays of dawn. He moved quickly, quietly, a few steps behind the Mongol hurrying toward his pickup, and watched him open the driver's door, reaching behind the seat, pulling out a rifle.

Right behind the Mongol now, Klug put the barrel of his pistol in the man's ribs and took his rifle while pushing him into the driver's seat and closing the door, all in one smooth motion.

He said, "Mr. Torrez. Listen up. I'll say this once."

Martin turned his eyes on him, listening.

Klug said, "You keep your hands right on top the wheel there and you won't get shot. I want you to think about what I say."

"Fuck you," said the Mongol.

"Mr. Martin," said Klug. "Remain calm," and brought up the rifle to shoot out the front tire. He plugged the rear tire, and then put a third one through the windshield from the inside for effect.

The Mongol looked up at him as he said, "You watch your back—"

He didn't finish the thought before Klug grabbed a fist full of the man's dyed blond hair and slammed the side of his face on the windowsill.

Klug bent down to look into the Mongol's face, bloody and wincing in pain, and said, "You stay clear of me. I'd eat you for breakfast, but your kind of fat only gives me gas."

As Klug walked quickly back to his jeep, he turned and put two more random shots into the big new pickup.

As he sped out onto the highway, the two drug suppliers he'd met at the bar turned into the driveway to the ranch.

"I didn't know he was in a motorcycle gang," said Karla, sobbing, and blowing her nose into the bandanna he'd passed to her.

"You mean the guy who got you into this mess?"

"He always drove around in a nice car. Such a gentleman, so generous, and clean cut. I thought he was a good man like you. Where's Sara?"

He drove on through the border patrol checkpoint. "Sweetie, you don't have to talk about it now. You just went through an ordeal. Rest. It's a couple hours back to Vegas, you haven't slept."

"It's so embarrassing," she said. "Poor choice of boyfriends." She leaned over toward him. He put his arm around her shoulders, a woman who wanted to be held. He sensed how upset she was. He felt it in her hands, warm and sweaty from tears and exhaustion. She raised her face to say, "I can't believe all this happened."

"Everyone makes mistakes," he said. "Don't be so hard on yourself."

"I should've known better."

"Sheila told me," he said.

"Told you what?"

"He didn't treat you well," he said. "What was his name? Golson…no Olson?"

"Most of the time," she said, "he was a prince who treated me like a princess. Other times, he did things, vulgar things, things

I'm ashamed of, and then talk to me bad, call me a whore and worse than that. And the last time I saw him, I told him I did not want to be with him again. He got so angry. I still have a knot on the back of my head where I fell and hit my head on a chair." She put her hand on the back of her head. "Here," she said. Her hair was a mess. She touched her scalp, fingers probing. "You want to feel it?"

With his eyes on the road and his left hand on the wheel, he moved his right hand from her shoulders to the spot she touched.

He tried to ignore what a beautiful woman she was, a dancer, like his wife, Sheila. He glanced down at her face, with the striking features of an American Indian. He noticed her dark skin and refined body. Her skirt had been torn open, the tops of her breasts shone in the moonlight. An unstoppable surge filled his groin, making him feel awkward in such a contradictory situation. She was so vulnerable, the damsel in distress he had rescued. Now the arousal made him feel like the criminal, not the hero, and she, once again, a victim.

"Took me more than six months dating him before I found out he was no good," she said, calm now, sipping spring water from a plastic bottle. “And his so-called business was buying cocaine from Mexico and selling it in Vegas.”

“He still around?” he asked.

“Who? Dart? I don’t know, never see him since we broke up,” she said. “You want some water?” She was practically whispering in his ear, holding up the open bottle.

“When was that?” he said and took a long drink.

“More than a week ago, why?”

Klug watched the road, silent for a moment.

“You think he made this happen?” she said.

“One hell of a coincidence, if not,” he said. “You haven’t seen him since you broke up? None of his friends? Nothing?”

“No, nothing” she said, “not until thugs grabbed me and Sara. How can we find Sara?”

She began to sob again and the crying tired her until she fell asleep, her head on his leg, her feet against his jeep’s door, her pantyhose torn at the toes and knees.

They rolled north and by the time the skyscrapers appeared on the Las Vegas horizon, the dawn broke the darkness.

"I never thought he'd be after me just because I stopped seeing him," she said as if crawling out of a bad dream, waking up as the day shone bright and Klug slowed down now that they exited the highway and moved into city traffic.

Karla lighted a cigarette from a pack she pulled out of a pocket in her skirt and blew a stream of smoke by him. "I made the mistake of living with him a couple of weeks. Any time we went out he acted like he owned me. Men look at me all the time, you know, like your wife; we're in good shape, take care of our looks. It drove Dart crazy any time a man looked at me. Got into a fight with one guy who tried to strike up a conversation with me. He hit him square in the face. What scared me away for good was when he hit me for dressing up nice when I went to an audition. He slapped me on the face and ripped open my blouse in public, on the sidewalk right outside his house. He screamed at me, 'What's wrong with you? Don't you know how to dress proper?'" She drew on the cigarette again and threw it out the window, as if she'd lost the taste for it. Klug was grateful that Sheila didn't smoke—he hated the smell of it. Smoke came out her mouth as she said, "The man is so jealous and possessive he'd stop by the dance studio to check on me."

"You have to give me his address," he said.

"You talk to him about me, he'll throw a fit," she said, sitting up straight now.

He rolled down his window, breathed in the cool air, waking up his senses after a long drive and a seemingly endless day and night. "You want to get your Sara back? We have to move fast. I'll take you to our house. Sheila is worried about you. Unless you want to go home?"

"Going back to my place is not much of an option," she said. "They could be waiting for me. What about the police?"

"I talked to them. I'll let them know that I brought you back but Sara is still missing. You can rest."

"She sure is a lucky girl to have a man like you," she said. "You should let me come with you. I can help you find Sara." She flirtatiously brushed back brushing her long dark hair with her hand.

"No," he said. "No offense, but I can work faster without you."

"Kris," she said, "you haven't slept. I did. I can drive you while you take a nap. Be reasonable. Let me go with you. I need to find Sara."

"I'm fine," he said. "I'll be back soon."

"Will you please call me when you have news?" she said.

When he let her off at his house, she gave him a little map she'd drawn on a piece of paper, and said, "Here's how to find Dart's place. You be careful. The man's crazy. You should get help from the police. You can't do this alone. By the way, he doesn't stay around his house much. He's usually out running around in his old pickup or on his big motorcycle. He spends a lot of time somewhere in southern California. I don't know where exactly. I heard him mention Laguna Beach once or twice when he was talking to his buddies on his cell phone, something about an old church. He hangs out with some kind of guys, motorcycle club of some sort. The little I heard about them, they sounded creepy."

When she opened the jeep's door, heading to his house, he took a quick look at her torn panty hose, her ripped skirt, her tousled blouse the red lace of her bra. A strange attraction, a sexual urge ran through him like a warm breeze. He pushed the notion out of his thoughts, blamed it on lack of sleep.

He drove off, not taking time to go into his house, see his wife, and freshen up. No time for that. The bad guys were out there with Sara. He couldn't have that on his conscience. He had to find them. Though it stayed with him, the image of Karla sleeping, her head on his thigh, her beautiful body, her soft voice.

"Karla told me her boyfriend spent a lot of his time somewhere around Laguna Beach," said Klug, going straight to the purpose of his call to Chavez.

"Out of my jurisdiction," said Chavez. "You let the local detectives do their job."

"Yeah, wait around for them to bring back Sara, like they did Karla?" he said.

"It's their job," said Chavez, "trained to do exactly that, not doing recon, sniping, explosives, or jumping outta airplanes."

"Too bad for them," he said. "I just passed Victorville. I'll be in their zone soon enough. You gonna help me or not?"

"Sure as hell will," Chavez was talking louder. The cell phone connection was crackling more and more as Klug was clearing the San Gabriels.

"But you gotta promise me," said Chavez.

"Promise you what?" said Klug, practically shouting over the bad connection.

"You work it out with the FBI. They'll soon be on this case now that it's an interstate kidnapping. And you'll not get yourself killed. Those biker guys are sociopaths."

Klug had already crossed the state line, passing through Barstow on Highway 15.

On his cell phone Chavez said, "Now it's something personal," in a disappointed voice.

"Has been since the start," Klug said. "Man tries to snatch your wife up from the street to sell her for drugs, that'd be personal."

He could hear Chavez saying, "I didn't give you that address either—"as the call was dropped.

Before their connection broke up, Klug got the address. Chavez had done a little search for Greco's name. Sure enough, they had a place in Laguna Beach.

***

Gypsy saw the dust rising up at the entrance to the driveway, moving up the grade, and told Greco somebody was coming. He quickly stood up from his wooden chair and put the two clear plastic bags of cocaine in a cabinet along with an electronic weighing device.

Standing close to the front door now, cracking it open, Gypsy peered out and said, “You know anybody drives an old jeep?”

“Let’s find out,” said Greco, walking to the door and out onto the porch with Gypsy right behind him, each playing it cool. Greco stepped down off the porch, grinning now because he recognized the man, and said, “My old buddy from Boy Scouts camp.”

***

Klug had to grin back at Greco. He recognized the undisciplined recruit he’d trained with when he got his basics out in the Mojave at Fort Irwin, right here in California.

Greco was standing there in the clear, dry morning air under a Joshua tree holding out his arms like they’d gone through all of WWII together. “Damn, look at you, still dressed like you just come outta basic." He hugged Klug, patting his back, Klug going along with the screwy charade.

As they stepped apart, Greco turned to Gypsy. "Now here's what a real soldier looks like, but fuck me in the ass, I plumb forgot your name. Kug, huh, Klug…ain't it?"

"That's right," he said, sizing up Gypsy, recalling how Chavez had that name down on a list of the motorcycle club members.

This one was looking straight back at Klug, giving him a dead-eyed look, showing he wasn't impressed for a second.

"I remember now," said Greco, "saw your picture in the newspaper. Story had it you shot down a little airplane, threw a grenade in it or some stupid-ass thing, Muslims trying to blow up Vegas."

"Probably confused with someone else," he said, taking off his hat, as they stood in the shade of the Joshua tree. "I'm just out scrounging for a little work. Government don't care much once they let us loose after doing our service."

"Man's gotta fend for himself, he wanna make it in this country," said Greco. "Gotta stay frosty. Dog eat dog nation."

"I talked to a guy in Mexicali who said you was in the business."

"And what business might that be?" Greco pulled out a box of Marlboros and lit one up, offering one to Klug.

"You know what I mean," he said, waving off the cigarette offer.

"What?" Gypsy stepped forward as if answering a boxing challenge.

"Buying snow down south, cut it, retail it here," he said.

"Who told you that?" Greco held up his cigarette in front of Gypsy to stand him down.

"Some half-wit in a bar just outside the town." He wiped the top of his head with his cloth fatigue hat. "I promised him I wouldn't tell anyone."

"Must a been Torrez's idiot son." Gypsy turned to look at Greco.

"Shut the fuck up." Greco flicked his cigarette into Gypsy's face. "Ignorant moron."

Gypsy and Greco stood silent for a second, giving each other the evil eye. Gypsy stepped back and looked down the dirt driveway.

"How you know this half-wit of yours didn't just send you to me to decide what to do with you?" Greco pulled out another Marlboro and lit it up.

"I can handle this dipshit," said Gypsy, trying to fix his slip of the tongue.

Greco didn't listen to him. "We know a Torrez down south but we don't know about any of this business about snow. Most people come live here in California just to get outta the snow."

Klug walked right past them up the porch steps, through the door, into the house. Greco and Gypsy were right behind him.

"The half-wit also told me about this house once being a church," Klug said as he began to scope out the front room, hoping maybe Sara might be there, simple as daylight. It was spare of furnishing—an old couch covered in plastic, yellowing from the years like some old folks must have lived here for decades. A couple of posters taped to the walls, pictures of naked women bending over motorcycles.

"You sure like choppers," he said and looked over at Greco.

"I also heard you got a little motorcycle club. What's that all about?"

"Freedom of the open road," Greco said.

"Freedom to keep us safe from the heathen Jews and Muslims, and those goddamn Scientologists, too." Gypsy talked like he was proud of his club and his purpose.

"What's with the tattoos," Klug said, stepping into the kitchen and noticing a couple of drops of dried blood on the dirty linoleum floor and a woman's sweater on the back of a chair.

"You ask questions, I give you that much," said Greco. "I'd say you walked into this house without invitation and now it's high time you walk on outta here."

Klug turned and walked back to the living room. "What about the Christians?" he asked.

"What about 'em?" Gypsy said.

"You mentioned just about everybody 'cept them."

"We are followers of Jesus and proud of it. God fearing," said Gypsy. "Only ones chosen by God now, don't you know? All that matters is you being God-chosen, nothing else counts. Don't matter much what a man does so long as he's God-chosen and follows Jesus. Look at Genghis Khan, man ruled the world ’cause God chose him. The man made babies with every woman he took to. A righteous Mongol. And God blessed him to prosper and multiply.”

“You two born again?”

“That’s right,” said Gypsy.

“You killed them Muslims, ones trying to blow up Vegas,” said Greco. “You must be a follower of Jesus, you got the fiery passion like Saint Paul. The one who said, and I quote, “Those who are not with the Lord Jesus are the enemies of the Christ.”

“Saint Paul said that, huh?” Klug stepped out on the porch, eying the dilapidated barn that stood several yards behind the house that looked like someone must have used it as a car shop a long time ago, what with the car parts rusting under the sun.

“You looking for employment?” said Greco. “We might be able to do something for you, but we have to put you through indoctrination and educate you about the holy word of Jesus Christ the Messiah. Our fellowship is organized and guided by the teachings of our Savior. We break you in, make you submit, lose your pride.”

“I’d like to learn more.” Klug walked toward his jeep.

“It takes time,” said Gypsy.

“We have to get to know you. You’d have to hang around for a year, learn the ropes of our way of life, serving our Lord, enjoying the free and open road. You’d have to clean things up, paint the church.”

“Come on around the side of the house here,” said Gypsy. “Got something to show you, a whole lot better than this beat-up jeep.”

The three of them walked around, the side of the house. Gypsy pointed to a rigid-frame chopper. “What do you think?”

“Nice,” said Klug. “A Harley.”

“You want it? It’s yours for $3,000.”

“I don’t have that kind of money.”

“You can work for it doing odd jobs for us. Start hanging around.”

“I’d like that.” said Klug. “My jeep hardly runs anymore. But I stay here, how do I eat? Like I say, I need a job.”

“You do good,” said Greco, “we’ll feed you, throw you a bone once in a while.”

"I got debts too," said Klug. "I need to join up with an outfit where I can make serious money and quick. I'd do pretty much anything and I'm capable."

"How we know you ain't a snitch or some such thing?" said Gypsy, stepping up into Klug's face.

"You're full of shit," he said, meeting Gypsy square and up close, face to face, smelling his breath of stale beer and crank smoke, aroma of putrid meat.

Not much of a boxer, telegraphing his swings, Gypsy threw the first punch, trying to hook Klug under the chin. Klug blocked his punch and jabbed him straight in the face. He reeled back on his heels and tripped, falling backward. Klug beat him in half a minute.

"Fuck," said Gypsy, holding up his head, trying to stop the blood from dripping. "You broke my nose." He stepped back into the house. Klug and Greco followed.

"Listen," said Klug, "I don't give a shit what it takes to cut into your operations and I don't know how I can prove myself to you guys, but I don't like being accused of something I don't do."

"Go on," said Greco to Gypsy, "stop your whining, and get us a couple shot glasses and a bottle of Johnny." He raised his voice.

"Clean glasses." Gypsy disappeared into the kitchen. Greco returned to Klug. "He just got released from Wasco, eager to get some action."

"Looks like it," said Klug.

"Went down three years on a cocaine conviction—bought some south of the border. All the cops found on him was a bag. He didn't convince the court he wasn't selling."

Now Klug lost all doubt that Greco was the one who drove Sara and Karla down to Mexicali. "There's good money hauling it up here."

"You talk like you done the business," said Greco.

"One more thing," said Klug. "They pay good money for young women down there."

"That so, listen, I got a—" Greco stopped and looked at Gypsy, who slid a bottle of Johnny Walker over the coffee table to them and placed three shot glasses down, his fingers in each one.

Greco shoved one of the glasses back. "You go on and clean the blood off your nose."

Gypsy looked up, eying the two men like he wanted to argue to have a shot. "Go on," said Greco, "clean up."

He passed a glass full to Klug and said, "He don't need to be into all my business."

The two men emptied their glasses with a quick nod.

"How you feel about that kind of trading?" said Greco, pouring out two more shots.

Klug gulped down the second shot, smooth, but made him swallow his spit once or twice, and said, "I need money, and that's one of the fastest ways."

"Listen," said Greco, "I got an opportunity for you—" He downed his shot.

"What's that?" said Klug.

"Something along these lines," said Greco.

"Right there in the Bible, from the Old Testament to Saint Paul, says woman must remain the dominion of men, says woman submit to men."

"I don't know much about that, but you sound like a scholar on the subject," Klug said.

"Don't get smart with me," said Greco.

"I didn't say it like that," said Klug.

They stood facing each other across the table, the whiskey bottle between them. Greco stood straight, military style, sucking it up and showing his size, a tad bigger than Klug, who played it cool, remembering why he was right there and then. He only shrugged. "Cut me in on your traffic and you'll see more action than ever before."

"I'll think about it," said Greco, walking him out to his jeep. "We hold church tonight, you come hang around, keep guard outside during our meeting, and you start work to earn that old bike."

"Spider called," said Gypsy the minute Greco stepped back into the house. "He tells that Torrez had trouble with that woman we sold him, she broke away, disappeared."

"To hell with Torrez," said Greco.

"Kiss your new friend good-bye?" said Gypsy.

Greco looked over at him. "You want your nose broke again?"

“Just a joke,” Gypsy said, waiting for Greco to sit at the table, to look at their plan.

“Here, look, we head straight down to T-town before dawn and head down Highway 5 and then west on the Mexico 1D Highway.”

“Spider confirmed the deal?” said Greco.

“The man has the cash. Some old retired rich guy lives on the beach, always wanted to own a seventeen year old. We got the place and time for delivery.”

Greco traced his finger along one of Gypsy’s pencil lines on the map. “That the place?”

”Yep, off the highway, ten miles of dirt road.”

“Right near the beach, no main roads,” said Greco. “Looks good. Let’s get the girl off our hands. Nothing but trouble.”

***

He was still in his jeep out on the gravel driveway. He hadn’t even started the engine. Just sitting there thinking about where they put Sara. He could look all over the region from Orange County, California to Mexico, or work his way into their operations and let them tell him.

That was when Greco stepped out on the porch to stand, hands in his pockets, a cigarette between his lips with its smoke curling up into the warm noon air. As soon as Greco noticed him in his jeep he walked over and said, “You still here?”

“You wanted me to work tonight,” said Klug.

“Looks like it.” Greco drew on his cigarette, blew the smoke over the top of Klug’s jeep. Standing close to his window. “Hey, I was wondering about one thing. When you were out there in the desert tracking down them rag heads, picking them off one at a time, they say you came close to killing a cop too?”

“Who says that?” he said.

“Everyone at Wasco was talking about it for months, a legend. They say you were aiming to kill the cop right along with those hajjis.”

“Not a cop,” said Klug, “A goddamn FBI agent—he did nothing but get in my way.”

"So what they say is true," said Greco. "You went on the warpath when you came back from Iraq."

"Maybe I'm still on one," he said, "like they say, you know, once a warrior always a—"

"Goddamn right," said Greco. "You can stay out around here. You seem like a good recruit. We might have work for you real soon. Got a business transaction down south. We'll need a lookout." Greco turned toward the house.

Klug asked, "What's a lookout do?"

"You get on-the-job training. We go down there to deliver a package. You stay out near the highway looking out for anyone coming. Got it?" said Greco.

Klug nodded and gave him a salute with two fingers and watched Greco walk back into the house.

The hot afternoon made him drowsy as he waited in his jeep, watching for something, anything. He had decided by now that Sara was in there somewhere, the house, the church, the barn. He'd find out soon enough. Lack of sleep over the last two days led him to take a little siesta. His thoughts drifted through his plans. He figured it was like a military objective to take apart this little band of amateur motorcycle gangsters, Angels, Mongols, shitheads, whatever. Looking at it without much emotion, he had worked his way in just as far as he needed.

He figured he must have gotten an hour of deep sleep because, when he woke up, his mouth and throat were parched, his head tilted up against the back of the driver's seat. He'd been breathing full throttle, mouth gaping wide open when the junk Cadillac drove up to the house. Before the dust settled, three young men jumped out of the car and bolted through the front door. It was their meeting, what Greco called "church."

During the emergency meeting, Greco spoke to his "devoted dudes," who gathered for another run to Mexicali. He was putting it on hold, Greco said. There was the matter of the young woman they had to settle first and that they had found a buyer down on the west side of Tijuana. There's an old creep says he'll pay eleven grand for her.

He told them he got news from Torrez down in Mexicali about the older woman they'd delivered. Torrez said a group of twenty men from a rival drug lord, El Conejo, raided his house, killed one of the women, and stole another. They found some gringo dead near the side of the road, his head cut off.

Spider chuckled at the story and said it was bullshit.

Greco only nodded in agreement.

"We gotta deliver this chick," said Greco. "Get that trouble maker off our hands."

"I just a soon spank her," said Spider, "crack open hér tight little cheeks and pump a gang bang."

"None of that," said Greco, "use whatever brains you got. We sell her, collect the cash, and are done with it, the sooner the better. She's a hot potato. People be looking for her."

"Damn straight," said Gypsy, who had just put his pistol back together after cleaning it up military style.

"Listen up;" said Greco. "This is the plan. Gypsy stays with me. We take the girl in my car. The rest of you load up in Spider's Caddie and head out now to the end of the driveway until we tell you to go. We stay in contact by cell phone. You stay ahead of us a mile or two."

"What about that newcomer hanging out there in the drive way?"

"He rides shotgun a mile behind us," said Greco.

"How you know he ain't a snitch?" said Gypsy, moving to the window, looking for Klug in his jeep.

"We'll find out soon enough," said Greco, handing an AK47 to Spider. "Nah, he's a straight up dude, just down on his luck."

Klug was hunched down on the porch below the front window, listening to the better part of Greco's plan. By the time Greco's loyal goons came out of the house and turned Spider's old Caddie down toward the long gravel driveway, he jumped back in his jeep. He gave him another two finger salute as their headlights shined on him while they passed by. He kept his headlights off as he followed a half mile behind them watching how their red taillights reflected off the Caddie's fishtail chrome. When they stopped a couple miles away from the house, he stopped too and walked up behind them, opening the back door where a seat was empty next to Bullet.

Before Spider knew what was happening he lit a cigarette, turned to Hog in the passenger seat next to him and said, “I don’t know why Greco wants the damn stranger tagging along. Nothing he can do for us.”

Hog looked and said to Klug, “The fuck you doing here?”

“Greco wanted me to ride with you, figured you could show me the ropes.” No sooner did he say that than he pulled up the shotgun that was lying on the floor and rested the barrel on the front seat between Hog’s shaved head and Spider’s tattooed neck, racked it, squeezed the trigger, and blew most of the windshield away.

The gangsters pressed their hands over their ears. Bullet grabbed the shotgun’s barrel, but Klug twisted it around to bust the stock square against Bullet’s ear, making him slump over unconscious. He racked the shotgun again, and Spider turned around to grab it.

Klug smacked him solid with the barrel across his bandaged nose with such a force that his head bounced off the car’s window, leaving it with a spider web of cracked glass. He then pushed the muzzle against the back of Hog's neck. "You reach into your friend's pocket and give me his cell phone, and then yours."

He dug into the pocket of his military cargo pants, pulled out two sets of handcuffs, and cuffed Bullet's hand to Spider's left hand. With the other set of bracelets he cuffed the chain of the first cuffs to the steering wheel and to Bullet's hand. He emptied the car of all cell phones and guns, put them all in the jeep, and pocketed the car keys, saying, "You boys sit tight. When I get the chance, I'll call 911 to get you some help."

He sped his jeep back up to the house and walked in through the front door in a casual manner, moving toward Greco who was sitting in the living room preparing to leave. He said, "I heard gunshots down the hill."

"We're ready to go," said Greco. "Probably just those numb nuts screwing around."

He followed Greco into the kitchen where he saw Gypsy rolling duct tape around Sara's wrists.

"She's a runaway," Gypsy said to Klug. "We caught her, and her daddy wants us to take her back down south." Gypsy slapped tape across Sara's mouth before she could say a word to Klug, who sat down at the kitchen table next to Sara as Gypsy moved to tape her ankles.

Greco stopped him, saying, "Gypsy, you go get the car ready, open the back door so we can lay her on the floor. Klug, here, can do her feet."

Before Gypsy disappeared out the front door, Greco sat down across the table from him as he bent over, reaching for the girl's ankles. In a flash, Klug sat up straight, stared Greco in the eyes and said, "You know damn well this is the end of the road, right here."

"The fuck you talking?" said Greco, pulling his pistol from behind his back, under his belt behind his back, laying it down on the table next to him.

Klug saw it was a Berretta nine.

"No dipshits allowed here," said Greco. "You can't handle the work, get the hell outta here."

"Oh," said Klug, "I can handle the work all right 'cept it ain't quite the kind you do."

"So, Gypsy was right, then?" said Greco. "Look at you threatening me when I got a gun, bullets with your name all over 'em. Is this the way you killed them rag heads out in the desert? Just sit down close up like having coffee at the kitchen table?"

"I told you already, mostly long distance, picking them off one by one."

Klug picked up a little steak knife that Gypsy was using to cut the tape. He carefully removed the tape from Sara's wrist as if Greco didn't matter.

"Yeah," said Greco, "back then you had your gun, what? A rifle?"

"Antique Winchester, kind you see in cowboy movies."

"Cowboys and Indians, huh?" said Greco as if he were enjoying the situation. He picked up his Berretta from the table, braced his hand on the table top, and pointed the gun straight at Klug.

"Now you're sitting at the table with nothing but a steak knife in your hand. What's your plan? Where's your gun this time?"

"Holstered," said Klug.

"You don't stand a chance in hell," said Greco.

"You can call this whole thing off," said Klug. "You'd stand to win 'cause you'd probably only get another couple years back up at Wasco. Maybe that for-profit corporation that runs the prison can straighten you out the next time around."

Greco shook his head. "Man, you're some kind of dude."

"Beretta's in your hand, but I'd have to pull," Klug said. "The way you want it?"

"Tell you what," said Greco, laying his pistol down. "I'll set mine down, give you some kind of cowboy's chance. What you packin' under your arm there?"

"You don't want to find out." Klug said.

"Tough cowpoke, huh?" said Greco with a chuckle. "How much action you see over there in the goddamn land of hajjis?"

"Enough to know not to talk about it."

"Vegas newspaper said you got some kind of dishonorable discharge. That right?"

"Don't believe what all them journalists say."

"You wanna have another shot of Johnny, that taste on your tongue all the way with you to the next life?" said Greco. He paused to look at Sara as she stood up to run, losing her nerve to stay still.

Klug saw her in the corner of his eye as watched Greco pick up his gun and turn toward her. He shot Greco dead center in the upper chest, the force of it throwing him backward out of his chair.

Klug stood up, squeezed Sara next to him, and moved with her against the kitchen wall next to the passageway. They waited for Gypsy, who ran into the kitchen following the gunshot, a pistol in his hand.

Klug didn't take time for another conversation. When Gypsy turned around after looking at Greco lying flat out, Klug shot him square in the chest, too.

He helped Sara out to his jeep, buckled her seat belt, and called his buddy Chavez, who didn't answer. So he left a voice message for him. "Chavez," Klug said, "send out help. Three punks are chained up inside an old gas guzzler at the same address gave me not a day ago."